W9-ANM-093

WITHDRAWN
NDSU

LEONID ANDREYEV.

Courtesy of The New York Times.

THE SEVEN WHO WERE HANGED.

A STORY

BY

LEONID ANDREYEV.

AUTHORIZED TRANSLATION FROM THE RUSSIAN BY

HERMAN BERNSTEIN.

NEW YORK:
J. S. OGILVIE PUBLISHING COMPANY,
57 ROSE STREET.

The Seven Who Were Hanged.

DEDICATION

To Count Leo N. Tolstoy
This Book is Dedicated
by
Leonid Andreyev

The Translation of this Story
Is Also Respectfully
Inscribed to
Count Leo N. Tolstoy
by
Herman Bernstein

FOREWORD

Leonid Andreyev, who was born in Oryol, in 1871, is the most popular, and next to Tolstoy, the most gifted writer in Russia to-day. Andreyev has written many important stories and dramas, the best known among which are "Red Laughter," "Life of Man," "To the Stars," "The Life of Vasily Fiveisky," "Eliazar," "Black Masks," and "The Story of the Seven Who Were Hanged."

In "Red Laughter" he depicted the horrors of war as few men had ever before done it. He dipped his pen into the blood of Russia and wrote the tragedy of the Manchurian war.

In his "Life of Man" Andreyev produced a great, imaginative "morality" play which has been ranked by European critics with some of the greatest dramatic masterpieces.

The story of "The Seven Who Were Hanged" is thus far his most important achievement. The keen psychological insight and the masterly simplicity with which Andreyev has penetrated and depicted each of the tragedies of the seven who were hanged place him in the same class as an artist with Russia's greatest masters of fiction, Dostoyevsky, Turgenev and Tolstoy.

I consider myself fortunate to be able to present to the English-reading public this remarkable work, which has already produced a profound impression in Europe and which, I believe, is destined for a long time to come to play an important part in opening the eyes of the world to the horrors perpetrated in Russia and to the violence and iniquity of the destruction of human life, whatever the error or the crime.

New York. HERMAN BERNSTEIN.

Fac-Simile of Leonid Andreyev's Letter to Herman Bernstein, Concerning the Story of "The Seven Who Were Hanged."

5/18 октября 1908 г.

- Я очень радъ, многоуважаемый г. Бернштейнъ что "Разсказъ о семи повѣшенныхъ" будутъ читать на англійскомъ языкѣ. Несчастье всѣхъ насъ въ томъ, что мы очень мало или совсѣмъ даже ничего не знаемъ другъ о другѣ - ни о душѣ, ни о жизни, ни о страданіяхъ ни о привычкахъ, наклонностяхъ и стремленіяхъ. И художественная литература, которой я имѣю честь служить тѣмъ и дорога мнѣ, что благороднѣйшей задачей своею ставитъ уничтожніе границъ и разстояній.

Какъ въ жесткую скорлупу, заключенъ каждый человѣкъ въ свою оболочку изъ тѣла, платья и жизни. Кто онъ? - объ этомъ мы только догадываемся; въ чемъ его радость и печаль? - объ этомъ мы только гадаемъ по его поступкамъ, часто загадочнымъ, по его смѣху и слезамъ, часто совершенно намъ не понятнымъ. И если мы, русскіе, живя въ тѣснотѣ и постоянной обидѣ, такъ плохо понимаемъ другъ друга, что казнимъ безжалостно тамъ, гдѣ надо только жалѣть или даже награждать, и награждаемъ въ тѣхъ случаяхъ, когда нужно карать пре зрѣніемъ и гнѣвомъ - то насколько же труднѣе Вашимъ соотечественникамъ понять далекую Россію? Пожалуй, не менѣе трудно, чѣмъ намъ, русскимъ, понять далекую Америку, о которой въ юности мы мечтаемъ и надъ которою такъ глубоко задумываемся въ зрѣломъ возрастѣ.

Еврейскіе погромы и голодъ; парламентъ и казни; грабежи и величайшее геройство; "черная сотня" и Левъ Толстой, - какое смѣшеніе лицъ и понятій, какой обильный и источникъ для всяческихъ недоразумѣній. Правда жизни испуганно молчитъ, и громко кричитъ ея наглая ложь, вызывая неотвязные и мучительные вопросы: кому сочувствовать? кому вѣрить? кого любить?

Въ разсказѣ о "Семи повѣшенныхъ" я попытался дать искренній и безпристрастный отвѣтъ на нѣкоторые изъ этихъ вопросовъ.

Насколько сдержанно и мягко отнесся я къ правящей и казнящей Россіи, объ этомъ лучше всего говоритъ сама русская цензура, допустившая книгу къ обращенію. Свидѣтельство достаточное, если вспомнить, сколько книгъ, брошюръ и газетъ нашло вѣчный покой въ мирной сѣни полицейскихъ участковъ, поднялось къ терпѣливому небу съ дымомъ и пламенемъ костра.

Но я и не стремился, впрочемъ, къ осужденію правительства, слава объ умѣ и добродѣтеляхъ котораго проникла далеко за предѣлы нашего несчастнаго отечества. Скромное и стыдливое не въ мѣру своихъ досто инствъ, оно искренне хотѣло бы уклониться и отъ этой чести, но, къ сожалѣнію, свободная печать Америки и Европы не пощадила его скромности и дала достаточно яркую картину славной дѣятельности его. Можетъ быть, здѣсь я и не правъ: очень возможно, что многіе честные люди Америки вѣрятъ въ чистоту намѣреній русскаго правительства - но это вопросъ столь сложный, что нуждается въ спеціальной разработкѣ, для которой необходимо и время и душевное спокойствіе. Но нѣтъ спокойной души въ Россіи.

Моей задачей было: указать на ужасъ и недопустимость смертной казни - при всякихъ условіяхъ. Великъ ужасъ казни, когда она постигаетъ людей мужественныхъ и честныхъ, виновныхъ лишь въ избыткѣ любви и чувства справедливости - здѣсь возмущается совѣсть. Но еще ужаснѣе веревка, когда она захлестываетъ горло людей слабыхъ и темныхъ. И какъ ни странно покажется это: съ меньшей скорбью истраданіемъ я смотрю на казнь революціонеровъ, подобныхъ Вернеру и Мусѣ, нежели на удавленіе этихъ этихъ темныхъ, скорбныхъ главою и сердцемъ убійцъ - Янсона и Цыганка. Даже послѣднему, безумному ужасу неотвратимо надвигающейся смерти могутъ противоставить: Вернеръ - свой просвѣщенный умъ и закаленную волю, Муся - свою чистоту и безгрѣшность......а чѣмъ могутъ отозваться слабые и грѣшные, какъ не безуміемъ, какъ не глубочайшимъ потрясеніемъ всѣхъ основъ своей человѣческой -

души? А ихнъ то,набивши руку на революціонарахъ,и вѣшаютъ теперь по всей Руси:гдѣ по одному,гдѣ сразу по десятку.Играющіе дѣти натыкаются на плохо зарытые трупы и собравшійся народъ съ ужасомъ смотритъ на торчащіе изъ-подъ земли лапти;прокуроры,присутствующіе при казняхъ,сходятъ съ ума и отвозятся въ больницу - а ихъ все вѣшаютъ,все вѣшаютъ...

Я глубоко благодаренъ Вамъ,г.Бернштейнъ, за трудъ,который Вы взяли на себя переводомъ этой печальной повѣсти. Зная чуткость американскаго народа,когда то пославшаго черезъ океанъ корабли съ хлѣбомъ для голодающей Россіи,я увѣренъ,что и здѣсь мои соотечественники ,въ своей злой и горькой долѣ, встрѣтятъ пониманіе и сочувствіе.И если моя правдивая повѣсть о семи изъ тысячъ повѣшенныхъ поможетъ разрушиться хоть одной перегородкѣ,отдѣляющей народъ отъ народа,человѣка отъ человѣка,душу отъ души - я почту себя счастливымъ.

Уважающій Васъ

Леонидъ Андреевъ

Ваммельсу,Финляндія.

INTRODUCTION

[Translation of the Foregoing Letter]

I am very glad that "The Story of the Seven Who Were Hanged" will be read in English. The misfortune of us all is that we know so little, even nothing, about one another—neither about the soul, nor the life, the sufferings, the habits, the inclinations, the aspirations of one another. Literature, which I have the honor to serve, is dear to me just because the noblest task it sets before itself is that of wiping out boundaries and distances.

As in a hard shell, every human being is enclosed in a cover of body, dress, and life. Who is man? We may only conjecture. What constitutes his joy or his sorrow? We may guess only by his acts, which are oft-times enigmatic; by his laughter and by his tears, which are often entirely incomprehensible to us. And if we, Russians, who live so closely together in constant misery, understand one another so poorly that we mercilessly put to death those who should be pitied or even rewarded, and reward those who should be punished by contempt and anger —how much more difficult is it for you Americans, to understand distant Russia? But then, it is just as difficult for us Russians to understand distant America, of which we dream in our youth and over which we ponder so deeply in our years of maturity.

The Jewish massacres and famine; a Parliament and executions; pillage and the greatest heroism; "The Black Hundred," and Leo Tolstoy—what a mixture of figures and conceptions, what a fruitful source for all kinds of misunderstandings! The truth of life stands aghast in silence, and its brazen falsehood is loudly shouting, uttering pressing, painful questions: "With whom shall I sympathize? Whom shall I trust? Whom shall I love?"

In the story of "The Seven Who Were

Hanged" I attempted to give a sincere and unprejudiced answer to some of these questions.

That I have treated ruling and slaughtering Russia with restraint and mildness may best be gathered from the fact that the Russian censor has permitted my book to circulate. This is sufficient evidence when we recall how many books, brochures and newspapers have found eternal rest in the peaceful shade of the police stations, where they have risen to the patient sky in the smoke and flame of bonfires.

But I did not attempt to condemn the Government, the fame of whose wisdom and virtues has already spread far beyond the boundaries of our unfortunate fatherland. Modest and bashful far beyond all measure of her virtues, Russia would sincerely wish to forego this honor, but unfortunately the free press of America and Europe has not spared her modesty, and has given a sufficiently clear picture of her glorious activities. Perhaps I am wrong in this: it is possible that many honest people in America believe in the purity of the Russian Government's intentions—but this question is of such importance that it requires a special treatment, for which it is necessary to have both time and calm of soul. But there is no calm soul in Russia.

My task was to point out the horror and the iniquity of capital punishment under any circumstances. The horror of capital punishment is great when it falls to the lot of courageous and honest people whose only guilt is their excess of love and the sense of righteousness—in such instances, conscience revolts. But the rope is still more horrible when it forms the noose around the necks of weak and ignorant people. And however strange it may appear, I look with a lesser grief and suffering upon the execution of the revolutionists, such as Werner and Musya, than upon the strangling of ignorant murderers, miserable in mind and heart, like Yanson and Tsiganok. Even the last mad horror of inevitably approaching execution Werner can offset by his enlightened mind and his iron will, and Musya, by her purity and her innocence. * * *

But how are the weak and the sinful to face it if not in madness, with the most violent shock to the very foundation of their souls? And these people, now that the Government has steadied its hands through its experience with the revolutionists, are being hanged throughout Russia—in some places one at a time, in others, ten at once. Children at play come upon badly buried bodies, and the crowds which gather look with horror upon the peasants' boots that are sticking out of the ground; prosecutors who have witnessed these executions are becoming insane and are taken away to hospitals—while the people are being hanged—being hanged.

I am deeply grateful to you for the task you have undertaken in translating this sad story. Knowing the sensitiveness of the American people, who at one time sent across the ocean, steamers full of bread for famine-stricken Russia, I am convinced that in this case our people in their misery and bitterness will also find understanding and sympathy. And if my truthful story about seven of the thousands who were hanged will help toward destroying at least one of the barriers which separate one nation from another, one human being from another, one soul from another soul, I shall consider myself happy.

Respectfully yours,

LEONID ANDREYEV.

THE SEVEN WHO WERE HANGED

CHAPTER I

AT ONE O'CLOCK, YOUR EXCELLENCY!

As the Minister was a very stout man, inclined to apoplexy, they feared to arouse in him any dangerous excitement, and it was with every possible precaution that they informed him that a very serious attempt upon his life had been planned. When they saw that he received the news calmly, even with a smile, they gave him, also, the details. The attempt was to be made on the following day at the time that he was to start out with his official report; several men, terrorists, whose plans had already been betrayed by a *provocateur,* and who were now under the vigilant surveillance of detectives, were to meet at one o'clock in the afternoon in front of his house, and, armed with bombs and revolvers, were to wait till he came out. There the terrorists were to be trapped.

"Wait!" muttered the Minister, perplexed. "How did they know that I was to leave the house at one o'clock in the afternoon with my report, when I myself learned of it only the day before yesterday?"

The Chief of the Guards stretched out his arms with a shrug.

"Exactly at one o'clock in the afternoon, your Excellency," he said.

Half surprised, half commending the work of the police, who had managed everything skilfully, the Minister shook his head, a morose smile upon his thick, dark lips, and still smiling obediently, and not desiring to interfere with the plans of the police, he hastily made ready, and went out to pass the night in some one else's hospitable palace. His wife and his two children were also removed from the dangerous house, before which the bomb-throwers were to gather upon the following day.

While the lights were burning in the palace, and courteous, familiar faces were bowing to him, smiling and expressing their concern, the dignitary experienced a sensation of pleasant excitement—he felt as if he had already received, or was soon to receive, some great and unexpected reward. But the people went away, the lights were extinguished, and through the mirrors, the lace-like and fantastic reflection of the electric lamps on the street, quivered across the ceiling and over the walls. A stranger in the house, with its paintings, its statues and its silence, the light—itself silent and indefinite—awakened painful thoughts in him as to the vanity of bolts and guards and walls. And then, in the dead of night, in the silence and solitude of a strange bedroom, a sensation of unbearable fear swept over the dignitary.

He had some kidney trouble, and whenever he grew strongly agitated, his face, his hands and his feet became swollen. Now, rising like a mountain of bloated flesh above the taut springs of the bed, he felt, with the anguish of a sick man, his swollen face, which seemed to him to belong to some one else. Unceasingly he kept thinking of the cruel fate which people were preparing for him. He recalled, one after another, all the recent horrible instances of bombs that had been thrown at men of even greater eminence than himself; he recalled how the bombs had torn bodies to pieces, had spattered brains over dirty brick walls, had knocked teeth from their roots. And influenced by these meditations, it seemed to him that his own stout, sickly body, outspread on the bed, was already experiencing the fiery shock of the explosion. He seemed to be able to feel his arms being severed from the shoulders, his teeth knocked out, his brains scattered into particles, his feet growing numb, lying quietly, their toes upward, like those of a dead man. He stirred with an effort, breathed loudly and coughed in order not to seem to himself to resemble a corpse in any way. He encouraged himself with the live noise of the grating springs, of the rustling blanket; and to assure himself that he was actually alive and not dead, he uttered in a bass voice, loudly and abruptly, in the silence and solitude of the bedroom:

"*Molodtsi! Molodtsi! Molodtsi!* (Good boys)!"

He was praising the detectives, the police, and the soldiers—all those who guarded his life, and who so opportunely and so cleverly had averted the assassination. But even though he stirred, even though he praised his protectors, even though he forced an unnatural smile, in order to express his contempt for the foolish, unsuccessful terrorists, he nevertheless did not believe in his safety, he was not sure that his life would not leave him suddenly, at once. Death, which people had devised for him, and which was only in their minds, in their intention, seemed to him to be already standing there in the room. It seemed to him that Death would remain standing there, and would not go away until those people had been captured, until the bombs had been taken from them, until they had been placed in a strong prison. There Death was standing in the corner, and would not go away—it could not go away, even as an obedient sentinel stationed on guard by a superior's will and order.

"At one o'clock in the afternoon, your Excellency!" this phrase kept ringing, changing its tone continually: now it was cheerfully mocking, now angry, now dull and obstinate. It sounded as if a hundred wound-up gramophones had been placed in his room, and all of them, one after another, were shouting with idiotic repetition the words they had been made to shout:

"At one o'clock in the afternoon, your Excellency!"

And suddenly, this one o'clock in the afternoon to-morrow, which but a short while ago was not in any way different from other hours, which was only a quiet movement of the hand along the dial of his gold watch, assumed an ominous finality, sprang out of the dial, began to live separately, stretched itself into an enormously huge black pole which cut all life in two. It seemed as if no other hours had existed before it and no other hours would exist after it—as if this hour alone, insolent and presumptuous, had a right to a certain peculiar existence.

"Well, what do you want?" asked the Minister angrily, muttering between his teeth.

The gramophone shouted:

"At one o'clock in the afternoon, your Excellency!" and the black pole smiled and bowed. Gnashing his teeth, the Minister rose in his bed to a sitting posture, leaning his face on the palms of his hands—he positively could not sleep on that dreadful night.

Clasping his face in his swollen, perfumed palms, he pictured to himself with horrifying clearness how on the following morning, not knowing anything of the plot against his life, he would have risen, would have drunk his coffee, not knowing anything, and then would have put on his coat in the hallway. And neither he, nor the doorkeeper who would have handed him his fur coat, nor the lackey who would have brought him the coffee, would have known that it was utterly useless to drink coffee, and to put on the coat, since a few instants later, everything—the fur coat and his body and the coffee within it—would be destroyed by an explosion, would be seized by death. The doorkeeper would have opened the glass door. . . . He, the amiable, kind, gentle doorkeeper, with the blue, typical eyes of a soldier, and with medals across his breast—he himself with his own hands would have opened the terrible door, opened it because he knew nothing. Everybody would have smiled because they did not know anything.

"Oho!" he suddenly said aloud, and slowly removed his hands from his face. Peering into the darkness, far ahead of him, with a fixed, strained look, he outstretched his hand just as slowly, felt the button on the wall and pressed it. Then he arose, and without putting on his slippers, walked in his bare feet over the rug in the strange, unfamiliar bedroom, found the button of another lamp upon the wall and pressed it. It became light and pleasant, and only the disarranged bed with the blanket, which had slipped off to the floor, spoke of the horror, not altogether past.

In his night-clothes, with his beard disheveled by his restless movements, with his angry eyes, the dignitary resembled any other angry old man who suffered with insomnia and shortness of breath. It was as if the death which people were preparing for him, had made him bare, had torn away from him the magnificence and splendor which had surrounded him—and it was hard to believe that it was he who had so much power, that his body was but an ordinary plain human body that must have perished terribly in the flame and roar of a monstrous explosion. Without dressing himself and not feeling the cold, he sat down in the first armchair he found, stroking his disheveled beard, and fixed his eyes in deep, calm thoughtfulness upon the unfamiliar plaster figures of the ceiling.

So that was the trouble! That was why he had trembled in fear and had become so agitated! That was why Death seemed to stand in the corner and would not go away, could not go away!

"Fools!" he said emphatically, with contempt.

"Fools!" he repeated more loudly, and turned his head slightly toward the door that those to whom he was referring might hear it. He was referring to those whom he had praised but a moment before, who in the excess of their zeal had told him of the plot against his life.

"Of course," he thought deeply, an easy, convincing idea arising in his mind. "Now that they have told me, I know, and feel terrified, but if I had not been told, I would not have known anything and would have drunk my coffee calmly. After that Death would have come—but then, am I so afraid of Death? Here have I been suffering with kidney trouble, and I must surely die from it some day, and yet I am not afraid—because I do not know anything. And those fools told me: 'At one o'clock in the afternoon, your Excellency!' and they thought I would be glad. But instead of that Death stationed itself in the corner and would not go away. It would not go away because it was my thought. It is not death that is terrible, but the knowledge of it: it would be utterly impossible to live if a man could know exactly and definitely the day and hour of his death. And the fools cautioned me: 'At one o'clock in the afternoon, your Excellency!' "

He began to feel light-hearted and cheerful, as if some one had told him that he was immortal, that he would never die. And, feeling himself again strong and wise amidst the herd of fools who had so stupidly and impudently broken into the mystery of the future, he began to think of the bliss of ignorance, and his thoughts were the painful thoughts of an old, sick man who had gone through endless experience. It was not given to any living being—man or beast—to know the day and hour of death. Here had he been ill not long ago and the physicians told him that he must expect the end, that he should make his final arrangements—

but he had not believed them and he remained alive. In his youth he had become entangled in an affair and had resolved to end his life; he had even loaded the revolver, had written his letters, and had fixed upon the hour for suicide—but before the very end he had suddenly changed his mind. It would always be thus—at the very last moment something would change, an unexpected accident would befall—no one could tell when he would die.

"At one o'clock in the afternoon, your Excellency!" those kind asses had said to him, and although they had told him of it only that death might be averted, the mere knowledge of its possibility at a certain hour again filled him with horror. It was probable that some day he should be assassinated, but it would not happen to-morrow—it would not happen to-morrow—and he could sleep undisturbed, as if he were really immortal. Fools—they did not know what a great law they had dislodged, what an abyss they had opened, when they said in their idiotic kindness: "At one o'clock in the afternoon, your Excellency!"

"No, not at one o'clock in the afternoon, your Excellency, but no one knows when. No one knows when! What?"

"Nothing," answered Silence, "nothing."

"But you did say something."

"Nothing, nonsense. I say: to-morrow, at one o'clock in the afternoon!"

There was a sudden, acute pain in his heart—and he understood that he would have neither sleep, nor peace, nor joy until that accursed black hour standing out of the dial should have passed. Only the shadow of the knowledge of something which no living being could know stood there in the corner, and that was enough to darken the world and envelop him with the impenetrable gloom of horror. The once disturbed fear of death diffused through his body, penetrated into his bones.

He no longer feared the murderers of the next day—they had vanished, they had been forgotten, they had mingled with the crowd of hostile faces and incidents which surrounded his life. He now feared something sudden and inevitable—an apoplectic stroke, heart failure, some foolish thin little vessel which might suddenly fail to withstand the pressure of the blood and might burst like a tight glove upon swollen fingers.

His short, thick neck seemed terrible to him. It became unbearable for him to look upon his short, swollen fingers—to feel how short they were and how they were filled with the moisture of death. And if before, when it was dark, he had had to stir in order not to resemble a corpse, now in the bright, cold, inimical, dreadful light he was so filled with horror that he could not move in order to get a cigarette or to ring for some one. His nerves were giving way. Each one of them seemed as if it were a bent wire, at the top of which there was a small head with mad, wide-open frightened eyes and a convulsively gaping, speechless mouth. He could not draw his breath.

Suddenly in the darkness, amidst the dust and cobwebs somewhere upon the ceiling, an electric bell came to life. The small, metallic tongue, agitatedly, in terror, kept striking the edge of the ringing cap, became silent—and again quivered in an unceasing, frightened din. His Excellency was ringing his bell in his own room.

People began to run. Here and there, in the shadows upon the walls, lamps flared up —there were not enough of them to give light, but there were enough to cast shadows. The shadows appeared everywhere; they rose in the corners, they stretched across the ceiling; tremulously clinging to each and every elevation, they covered the walls. And it was hard to understand where all these innumerable, deformed silent shadows—voiceless souls of voiceless objects—had been before.

A deep, trembling voice said something loudly. Then the doctor was hastily summoned by telephone; the dignitary was collapsing. The wife of his Excellency was also called.

CHAPTER II

CONDEMNED TO BE HANGED

EVERYTHING befell as the police had foretold. Four terrorists, three men and a woman, armed with bombs, infernal machines and revolvers, were seized at the very entrance of the house, and another woman was later found and arrested in the house where the conspiracy had been hatched. She was its mistress. At the same time a great deal of dynamite and half finished bomb explosives were seized. All those arrested were very young; the eldest of the men was twenty-eight years old, the younger of the women was only nineteen. They were tried in the same fortress in which they were imprisoned after the arrest; they were tried swiftly and secretly, as was done during that unmerciful time.

At the trial all of them were calm, but very serious and thoughtful. Their contempt for the judges was so intense that none of them wished to emphasize his daring by even a superfluous smile or by a feigned expression of cheerfulness. Each was simply as calm as was necessary to hedge in his soul, from curious, evil and inimical eyes, the great gloom that precedes death.

Sometimes they refused to answer questions; sometimes they answered, briefly, simply and precisely, as though they were answering not the judge, but statisticians, for the purpose of supplying information for particular special tables. Three of them, one woman and two men, gave their real names, while two others refused and thus remained unknown to the judges.

They manifested for all that was going on at the trial a certain curiosity, softened, as though through a haze, such as is peculiar to persons who are very ill or are carried away by some great, all-absorbing idea. They glanced up occasionally, caught some word in the air more interesting than the others, and then resumed the thought from which their attention had been distracted.

The man who was nearest to the judges called himself Sergey Golovin, the son of a retired colonel, himself an ex-officer. He was still a very young, light-haired, broad-shouldered man, so strong that neither the prison nor the expectation of inevitable death could remove the color from his cheeks and the expression of youthful, happy frankness from his blue eyes. He kept energetically tugging at his bushy, small beard, to which he had not become accustomed, and continually blinking, kept looking out of the window.

It was toward the end of winter, when amidst the snowstorms and the gloomy, frosty days, the approaching spring sent as a forerunner a clear, warm, sunny day, or but an hour, yet so full of spring, so eagerly young and beaming that sparrows on the streets lost their wits for joy, and people seemed almost as intoxicated. And now the strange and beautiful sky could be seen through an upper window which was dust-covered and unwashed since the last summer. At first sight the sky seemed to be milky-gray—smoke-colored—but when you looked longer the dark blue color began to penetrate through the shade, grew into an ever deeper blue—ever brighter, ever more intense. And the fact that it did not reveal itself all at once, but hid itself chastely in the smoke of transparent clouds, made it as charming as the girl you love. And Sergey Golovin looked at the sky, tugged at his beard, blinked now one eye, now the other, with its long, curved lashes, earnestly pondering over something. Once he began to move his fingers rapidly and thoughtlessly, knitted his brow in some joy, but then he glanced about and his joy died out like a spark which is stepped upon. Almost instantly an earthen, deathly blue, without first changing into pallor, showed through the color of his cheeks. He clutched his downy hair, tore their roots painfully with his fingers, whose tips had turned white. But the joy of life and spring was stronger, and a few minutes later his frank young face was again yearning toward the spring sky.

The young, pale girl, known only by the name of Musya, was also looking in the same direction, at the sky. She was younger than Golovin, but she seemed older in her gravity and in the darkness of her open, proud eyes. Only her very thin, slender neck, and her delicate girlish hands spoke of her youth; but in addition there was that ineffable something, which is youth itself, and which sounded so distinctly in her clear, melodious voice, tuned irreproachably like a precious instrument, every simple word, every exclamation giving evidence of its musical timbre. She was very pale, but it was not a deathly pallor, but that peculiar warm whiteness of a person within whom, as it were, a great, strong fire is burning, whose body glows transparently like fine Sèvres porcelain. She sat almost motionless, and only at times she touched with an imperceptible movement of her fingers the circular mark on the middle finger of her right hand, the mark of a ring which had been recently removed.

She gazed at the sky without caressing kindness or joyous recollections—she looked at it simply because in all the filthy, official hall the blue bit of sky was the most beautiful, the purest, the most truthful object, and the only one that did not try to search hidden depths in her eyes.

The judges pitied Sergey Golovin; her they despised.

Her neighbor, known only by the name of Werner, sat also motionless, in a somewhat affected pose, his hands folded between his knees. If a face may be said to look like a false door, this unknown man closed his face like an iron door and bolted it with an iron lock. He stared motionlessly at the dirty wooden floor, and it was impossible to tell whether he was calm or whether he was intensely agitated, whether he was thinking of something, or whether he was listening to the testimony of the detectives as presented to the court. He was not tall in stature. His features were refined and delicate. Tender and handsome, so that he reminded you of a moonlit night in the South near the seashore, where the cypress trees throw their dark shadows, he at the same time gave the impression of tremendous, calm power, of invincible firmness, of cold and audacious courage. The very politeness with which he gave brief and precise answers seemed dangerous, on his lips, in his half bow. And if the prison garb looked upon the others like the ridiculous costume of a buffoon, upon him it was not noticeable, so foreign was it to his personality. And although the other terrorists had been seized with bombs and infernal machines upon them, and Werner had had but a black revolver, the judges for some reason regarded him as the leader of the others and treated him with a certain deference, although succinctly and in a business-like manner.

The next man, Vasily Kashirin, was torn between a terrible, dominating fear of death and a desperate desire to restrain the fear and not betray it to the judges. From early morning, from the time they had been led into court, he had been suffocating from an intolerable palpitation of his heart. Perspiration came out in drops all along his forehead; his hands were also perspiring and cold, and his cold, sweat-covered shirt clung to his body, interfering with the freedom of his movements. With a supernatural effort of will-power he forced his fingers not to tremble, his voice to be firm and distinct, his eyes to be calm. He saw nothing about him; the voices came to him as through a mist, and it was to this mist that he made his desperate efforts to answer firmly, to answer loudly. But having answered, he immediately forgot question as well as answer, and was again struggling with himself silently and terribly. Death was disclosed in him so clearly that the judges avoided looking at him. It was hard to define his age, as is the case with a corpse which has begun to decompose. According to his passport, he was only twenty-three years old. Once or twice Werner quietly touched his knee with his hand, and each time Kashirin spoke shortly:

"Never mind!"

The most terrible sensation was when he

was suddenly seized with an insufferable desire to cry out, without words, the desperate cry of a beast. He touched Werner quickly, and Werner, without lifting his eyes, said softly:

"Never mind, Vasya. It will soon be over."

And embracing them all with a motherly, anxious look, the fifth terrorist, Tanya Kovalchuk, was faint with alarm. She had never had any children; she was still young and red-cheeked, just as Sergey Golovin, but she seemed as a mother to all of them: so full of anxiety, of boundless love were her looks, her smiles, her sighs. She paid not the slightest attention to the trial, regarding it as though it were something entirely irrelevant, and she listened only to the manner in which the others were answering the questions, to hear whether the voice was trembling, whether there was fear, whether it was necessary to give water to any one.

She could not look at Vasya in her anguish and only wrung her fingers silently. At Musya and Werner she gazed proudly and respectfully, and she assumed a serious and concentrated expression, and then tried to transfer her smile to Sergey Golovin.

"The dear boy is looking at the sky. Look, look, my darling!" she thought about Golovin.

"And Vasya! What is it? My God, my God! What am I to do with him? If I should speak to him I might make it still worse. He might suddenly start to cry."

So like a calm pond at dawn, reflecting every hastening, passing cloud, she reflected upon her full, gentle, kind face every swift sensation, every thought of the other four. She did not give a single thought to the fact that she, too, was upon trial, that she, too, would be hanged; she was entirely indifferent to it. It was in her house that the bombs and the dynamite had been discovered, and, strange though it may seem, it was she who had met the police with pistol-shots and had wounded one of the detectives in the head.

The trial ended at about eight o'clock, when it had become dark. Before Musya's and Golovin's eyes the sky, which had been turning ever bluer, was gradually losing its tint, but it did not turn rosy, did not smile softly as in summer evenings, but became muddy, gray, and suddenly grew cold, wintry. Golovin heaved a sigh, stretched himself, glanced again twice at the window, but the cold darkness of the night alone was there; then continuing to tug at his short beard, he began to examine with childish curiosity the judges, the soldiers with their muskets, and he smiled at Tanya Kovalchuk. When the sky had darkened Musya calmly, without lowering her eyes to the ground, turned them to the corner where a small cobweb was quivering from the imperceptible radiations of the steam heat, and thus she remained until the sentence was pronounced.

After the verdict, having bidden good-by to their frock-coated lawyers, and evading each other's helplessly confused, pitying and guilty eyes, the convicted terrorists crowded in the doorway for a moment and exchanged brief words.

"Never mind, Vasya. Everything will be over soon," said Werner.

"I am all right, brother," Kashirin replied loudly, calmly and even somewhat cheerfully. And indeed, his face had turned slightly rosy, and no longer looked like that of a decomposing corpse.

"The devil take them; they've hanged us," Golovin cursed quaintly.

"That was to be expected," replied Werner calmly.

"To-morrow the sentence will be pronounced in its final form and we shall all be placed together," said Tanya Kovalchuk consolingly. "Until the execution we shall all be together."

Musya was silent. Then she resolutely moved forward.

CHAPTER III

WHY SHOULD I BE HANGED?

Two weeks before the terrorists had been tried the same military district court, with a different set of judges, had tried and condemned to death by hanging Ivan Yanson, a peasant.

Ivan Yanson was a workman for a well-to-do farmer, in no way different from other workmen. He was an Esthonian by birth, from Vezenberg, and in the course of several years, passing from one farm to another, he had come close to the capital. He spoke Russian very poorly, and as his master was a Russian, by name Lazarev, and as there were no Esthonians in the neighborhood, Yanson had practically remained silent for almost two years. In general, he was apparently not inclined to talk, and was silent not only with human beings, but even with animals. He would water the horse in silence, harness it in silence, moving about it, slowly and lazily, with short, irresolute steps, and when the horse, annoyed by his manner, would begin to frolic, to become capricious, he would beat it in silence with a heavy whip. He would beat it cruelly, with stolid, angry persistency, and when this happened at a time when he was suffering from the aftereffects of a carouse, he would work himself into a frenzy. At such times the crack of the whip could be heard in the house, with the frightened, painful pounding of the horse's hoofs upon the board floor of the barn. For beating the horse his master would beat Yanson, but then, finding that he could not be reformed, paid no more attention to him.

Once or twice a month Yanson became intoxicated, usually on those days when he took his master to the large railroad station, where there was a refreshment bar. After leaving his master at the station, he would drive off about half a verst away, and there, stalling the sled and the horse in the snow on the side of the road, he would wait until the train had gone. The sled would stand sideways, almost overturned, the horse standing with widely spread legs up to his belly in a snow-bank, from time to time lowering his head to lick the soft, downy snow, while Yanson would recline in an awkward position in the sled as if dozing away. The unfastened ear-lappets of his worn fur cap would hang down like the ears of a setter, and the moist sweat would stand under his little reddish nose.

Soon he would return to the station, and would quickly become intoxicated.

On his way back to the farm, the whole ten versts, he would drive at a fast gallop. The little horse, driven to madness by the whip, would rear, as if possessed by a demon; the sled would sway, almost overturn, striking against poles, and Yanson, letting the reins go, would half sing, half exclaim abrupt, meaningless phrases in Esthonian. But more often he would not sing, but with his teeth gritted together in an onrush of unspeakable rage, suffering and delight, he would drive silently on as though blind. He would not notice those who passed him, he would not call to them to look out, he would not slacken his mad pace, either at the turns of the road or on the long slopes of the mountain roads. How it happened at such times that he crushed no one, how he himself was never dashed to death in one of these mad rides, was inexplicable.

He would have been driven from this place, as he had been driven from other places, but he was cheap and other workmen were not better, and thus he remained there two years. His life was uneventful. One day he received a letter, written in Esthonian, but as he himself was illiterate, and as the others did not understand Esthonian, the letter remained unread; and as if not understanding that the letter might bring him tidings from his native home, he flung it into the manure with a certain savage, grim indifference. At one time Yanson tried to make love to the cook, but he was not successful, and was rudely rejected and ridiculed. He was short in stature, his face was freckled, and his small, sleepy eyes were somewhat of an indefinite color. Yanson took his failure indifferently, and never again bothered the cook.

But while Yanson spoke but little, he was listening to something all the time. He heard the sounds of the dismal, snow-covered fields, with their heaps of frozen manure resembling rows of small, snow-covered graves, the sounds of the blue, tender distance, of the buzzing telegraph wires, and the conversation of other people. What the fields and telegraph wires spoke to him he alone knew, and the conversation of the people were disquieting, full of rumors about murders and robberies and arson. And one night he heard in the neighboring village the little church bell ringing faintly and helplessly, and the crackling of the flames of a fire. Some vagabonds had plundered a rich farm, had killed the master and his wife, and had set fire to the house.

And on their farm, too, they lived in fear; the dogs were loose, not only at night, but also during the day, and the master slept with a gun by his side. He wished to give such a gun to Yanson, only it was an old one with one barrel. But Yanson turned the gun about in his hand, shook his head and declined it. His master did not understand the reason and scolded him, but the reason was that Yanson had more faith in the power of his Finnish knife than in the rusty gun.

"It would kill me," he said, looking at his master sleepily with his glassy eyes, and the master waved his hand in despair.

"You fool! Think of having to live with such workmen!"

And this same Ivan Yanson, who distrusted a gun, one winter evening, when the other workmen had been sent away to the station, committed a very complicated attempt at robbery, murder and rape. He did it in a surprisingly simple manner. He locked the cook in the kitchen, lazily, with the air of a man who is longing to sleep, walked over to his master from behind and swiftly stabbed him several times in the back with his knife. The master fell unconscious, and the mistress began to run about, screaming, while Yanson, showing his teeth and brandishing his knife, began to ransack the trunks and the chests of drawers. He found the money he sought, and then, as if noticing the mistress for the first time, and as though unexpectedly even to himself, he rushed upon her in order to violate her. But as he had let his knife drop to the floor, the mistress proved stronger than he, and not only did not allow him to harm her, but almost choked him into unconsciousness. Then the master on the floor turned, the cook thundered upon the door with the oven-fork, breaking it open, and Yanson ran away into the fields. He was caught an hour later, kneeling down behind the corner of the barn, striking one match after another, which would not ignite, in an attempt to set the place on fire.

A few days later the master died of blood poisoning, and Yanson, when his turn among other robbers and murderers came, was tried and condemned to death. In court he was the same as always; a little man, freckled, with sleepy, glassy eyes. It seemed as if he did not understand in the least the meaning of what was going on about him; he appeared to be entirely indifferent. He blinked his white eyelashes, stupidly, without curiosity; examined the sombre, unfamiliar courtroom, and picked his nose with his hard, shriveled, unbending finger. Only those who had seen him on Sundays at church would have known that he had made an attempt to adorn himself. He wore on his neck a knitted, muddy-red shawl, and in places had dampened the hair of his head. Where the hair was wet it lay dark and smooth, while on the other side it stuck up in light and sparse tufts, like straws upon a hail-beaten, wasted meadow.

When the sentence was pronounced—death by hanging—Yanson suddenly became agitated. He reddened deeply and began to tie and untie the shawl about his neck as though it were choking him. Then he waved his arms stupidly and said, turning to the judge who had not read the sentence, and pointing with his finger at the judge who read it:

"He said that I should be hanged."

"Who do you mean?" asked the presiding judge, who had pronounced the sentence in a deep, bass voice. Every one smiled; some tried to hide their smiles behind their mustaches and their papers. Yanson pointed his index finger at the presiding judge and answered angrily, looking at him askance:

"You!"

"Well?"

Yanson again turned his eyes to the judge who had been silent, restraining a smile, whom he felt to be a friend, a man who had nothing to do with the sentence, and repeated:

"He said I should be hanged. Why must I be hanged?"

"Take the prisoner away."

But Yanson succeeded in repeating once more, convincingly and weightily:

"Why must I be hanged?"

He looked so absurd, with his small, angry face, with his outstretched finger, that even the soldier of the convoy, breaking the rule, said to him in an undertone as he led him away from the courtroom:

"You are a fool, young man!"

"Why must I be hanged?" repeated Yanson stubbornly.

"They'll swing you up so quickly that you'll have no time to kick."

"Keep still!" cried the other convoy angrily. But he himself could not refrain from adding:

"A robber, too! Why did you take a human life, you fool? You must hang for that!"

"They might pardon him," said the first soldier, who began to feel sorry for Yanson.

"Oh, yes! They'll pardon people like him, will they? Well, we've talked enough."

But Yanson had become silent again.

He was again placed in the cell in which he had already sat for a month and to which he had grown accustomed, just as he had become accustomed to everything: to blows, to vodka, to the dismal, snow-covered fields, with their snow-heaps resembling graves.

And now he even began to feel cheerful when he saw his bed, the familiar window with the grating, and when he was given something to eat—he had not eaten anything since morning. He had an unpleasant recollection of what had taken place in the court, but of that he could not think—he was unable to recall it. And death by hanging he could not picture to himself at all.

Although Yanson had been condemned to death, there were many others similarly sentenced, and he was not regarded as an important criminal. They spoke to him accordingly, with neither fear nor respect, just as they would speak to prisoners who were not to be executed. The warden, on learning of the verdict, said to him:

"Well, my friend, they've hanged you!"

"When are they going to hang me?" asked Yanson distrustfully. The warden meditated a moment.

"Well, you'll have to wait—until they can get together a whole party. It isn't worth bothering for one man, especially for a man like you. It is necessary to work up the right spirit."

"And when will that be?" persisted Yanson. He was not at all offended that it was not worth while to hang him alone. He did not believe it, but considered it as an excuse for postponing the execution, preparatory to revoking it altogether. And he was seized with joy; the confused, terrible moment, of which it was so painful to think, retreated far into the distance, becoming fictitious and improbable, as death always seems.

"When? When?" cried the warden, a dull, morose old man, growing angry. "It isn't like hanging a dog, which you take behind the barn—and it is done in no time. I suppose you would like to be hanged like that, you fool!"

"I don't want to be hanged," and suddenly Yanson frowned strangely. "He said that I should be hanged, but I don't want it."

And perhaps for the first time in his life he laughed, a hoarse, absurd, yet gay and joyous laughter. It sounded like the cackling of a goose, Ga-ga-ga! The warden looked at him in astonishment, then knit his brow sternly. This strange gayety of a man who was to be executed was an offence to the prison, as well as to the very executioner; it made them appear absurd. And suddenly, for the briefest instant, it appeared to the old warden, who had passed all his life in the prison, and who looked upon its laws as the laws of nature, that the prison and all the life within it was something like an insane asylum, in which he, the warden, was the chief lunatic.

"Pshaw! The devil take you!" and he spat aside. "Why are you giggling here? This is no dramshop!"

"And I don't want to be hanged—ga-ga-ga!" laughed Yanson.

"Satan!" muttered the inspector, feeling the need of making the sign of the cross.

This little man, with his small, wizened face—he resembled least of all the devil—
face—he resembled least of all the devil—
but there was that in his silly giggling which the prison. If he laughed longer, it seemed to the warden as if the walls might fall

asunder, the grating melt and drop out, as if the warden himself might lead the prisoners to the gates, bowing and saying: "Take a walk in the city, gentlemen; or perhaps some of you would like to go to the village?"

"Satan!"

But Yanson had stopped laughing, and was now winking cunningly.

"You had better look out!" said the warden, with an indefinite threat, and he walked away, glancing back of him.

Yanson was calm and cheerful throughout the evening. He repeated to himself, "I shall not be hanged," and it seemed to him so convincing, so wise, so irrefutable, that it was unnecessary to feel uneasy. He had long forgotten about his crime, only sometimes he regretted that he had not been successful in attacking his master's wife. But he soon forgot that, too.

Every morning Yanson asked when he was to be hanged, and every morning the warden answered him angrily:

"Take your time, you devil! Wait!" and

he would walk off quickly before Yanson could begin to laugh.

And from these monotonously repeated words, and from the fact that each day came, passed and ended as every ordinary day had passed, Yanson became convinced that there would be no execution. He began to lose all memory of the trial, and would roll about all day long on his cot, vaguely and happily dreaming about the white melancholy fields, with their snow-mounds, about the refreshment bar at the railroad station, and about other things still more vague and bright. He was well fed in the prison, and somehow he began to grow stout rapidly and to assume airs.

"Now she would have liked me," he thought of his master's wife. "Now I am stout—not worse-looking than the master."

But he longed for a drink of vodka, to drink and to take a ride on horseback, to ride fast, madly.

When the terrorists were arrested the news of it reached the prison. And in answer to

Yanson's usual question, the warden said eagerly and unexpectedly:

"It won't be long now!"

He looked at Yanson calmly with an air of importance and repeated:

"It won't be long now. I suppose in about a week."

Yanson turned pale, and as though falling asleep, so turbid was the look in his glassy eyes, asked:

"Are you joking?"

"First you could not wait, and now you think I am joking. We are not allowed to joke here. You like to joke, but we are not allowed to," said the warden with dignity as he went away.

Toward evening of that day Yanson had already grown thinner. His skin, which had stretched out and had become smooth for a time, was suddenly covered with a multitude of small wrinkles, and in places it seemed even to hang down. His eyes became sleepy, and all his motions were now so slow and languid as though each turn of the head, each move of the fingers, each step of the foot were a complicated and cumbersome undertaking which required very careful deliberation. At night he lay on his cot, but did not close his eyes, and thus, heavy with sleep, they remained open until morning.

"Aha!" said the warden with satisfaction, seeing him on the following day. "This is no dramshop for you, my dear!"

With a feeling of pleasant gratification, like a scientist whose experiment had proved successful again, he examined the condemned man closely and carefully from head to foot. Now everything would go along as necessary. Satan was disgraced, the sacredness of the prison and the execution was re-established, and the old man inquired condescendingly, even with a feeling of sincere pity:

"Do you want to meet somebody or not?"

"What for?"

"Well, to say good-by! Have you no mother, for instance, or a brother?"

"I must not be hanged," said Yanson softly, and looked askance at the warden. "I don't want to be hanged."

The warden looked at him and waved his hand in silence.

Toward evening Yanson grew somewhat calmer.

The day had been so ordinary, the cloudy winter sky looked so ordinary, the footsteps of people and their conversation on matters of business sounded so ordinary, the smell of the sour soup of cabbage was so ordinary, customary and natural that he again ceased believing in the execution. But the night became terrible to him. Before this Yanson had felt the night simply as darkness, as an especially dark time, when it was necessary to go to sleep, but now he began to be aware of its mysterious and uncanny nature. In order not to believe in death, it was necessary to hear and see and feel ordinary things about him, footsteps, voices, light, the soup of sour cabbage. But in the dark everything was unnatural; the silence and the darkness were in themselves something like death.

And the longer the night dragged the more dreadful it became. With the ignorant innocence of a child or a savage, who believe everything possible, Yanson felt like crying to the sun: "Shine!" He begged, he implored that the sun should shine, but the night drew its long, dark hours remorselessly over the earth, and there was no power that could hasten its course. And this impossibility, arising for the first time before the weak consciousness of Yanson, filled him with terror. Still not daring to realize it clearly, he already felt the inevitability of approaching death, and felt himself making the first step upon the gallows, with benumbed feet.

Day quieted him, but night again filled him with fear, and so it was until one night when he realized fully that death was inevitable, that it would come in three days at dawn with the sunrise.

He had never thought of what death was, and it had no image to him—but now he realized clearly, he saw, he felt that it had entered his cell and was looking for him, groping about with its hands. And to save himself, he began to run wildly about the room.

But the cell was so small that it seemed

that its corners were not sharp but dull, and that all of them were pushing him into the center of the room. And there was nothing behind which to hide. And the door was locked. And it was dark. Several times he struck his body against the walls, making no sound, and once he struck against the door—it gave forth a dull, empty sound. He stumbled over something and fell upon his face, and then he felt that IT was going to seize him. Lying on his stomach, holding to the floor, hiding his face in the dark, dirty asphalt, Yanson howled in terror. He lay and cried at the top of his voice until some one came. And when he was lifted from the floor and seated upon the cot, and cold water was poured over his head, he still did not dare open his tightly closed eyes. He opened one eye, and noticing some one's boot in one of the corners of the room, he commenced crying again.

But the cold water began to produce its effect in bringing him to his senses. To help the effect, the warden on duty, the same old man, administered medicine to Yanson in the form of several blows upon the head. And this sensation of life returning to him really drove the fear of death away. Yanson opened his eyes, and then, his mind utterly confused, he slept soundly for the remainder of the night. He lay on his back, with mouth open, and snored loudly, and between his lashes, which were not tightly closed, his flat, dead eyes, which were upturned so that the pupil did not show, could be seen.

Later, everything in the world—day and night, footsteps, voices, the soup of sour cabbage, produced in him a continuous terror, plunging him into a state of savage uncomprehending astonishment. His weak mind was unable to combine these two things which so monstrously contradicted each other—the bright day, the odor and taste of cabbage—and the fact that two days later he must die. He did not think of anything. He did not even count the hours, but simply stood in mute stupefaction before this contradiction which tore his brain in two. And he became evenly pale, neither white nor redder in parts, and appeared to be calm. Only he ate nothing and ceased sleeping altogether. He sat all night long on a stool, his legs crossed under him, in fright. Or he walked about in his cell, quietly, stealthily, and sleepily looking about him on all sides. His mouth was half-open all the time, as though from incessant astonishment, and before taking the most ordinary thing into his hands, he would examine it stupidly for a long time, and would take it distrustfully.

When he became thus, the wardens as well as the sentinel who watched him through the little window, ceased paying further attention to him. This was the customary condition of prisoners, and reminded the wardens of cattle being led to slaughter after a staggering blow.

"Now he is stunned, now he will feel nothing until his very death," said the warden, looking at him with experienced eyes. "Ivan! Do you hear? Ivan!"

"I must not be hanged," answered Yanson, in a dull voice, and his lower jaw again drooped.

"You should not have committed murder.

You would not be hanged then," answered the chief warden, a young but very important-looking man with medals on his chest. "You committed murder, yet you do not want to be hanged?"

"He wants to kill human beings without paying for it. Fool! fool!" said another.

"I don't want to be hanged," said Yanson.

"Well, my friend, you may want it or not, that's your affair," replied the chief warden indifferently. "Instead of talking nonsense, you had better arrange your affairs. You still have something."

"He has nothing. One shirt and a suit of clothes. And a fur cap! A sport!"

Thus time passed until Thursday. And on Thursday, at midnight a number of people entered Yanson's cell, and one man, with shoulder-straps, said:

"Well, get ready. We must go."

Yanson, moving slowly and drowsily as before, put on everything he had and tied his muddy-red muffler about his neck. The man with shoulder-straps, smoking a cigarette, said to some one while watching Yanson dress:

"What a warm day this will be. Real spring."

Yanson's small eyes were closing; he seemed to be falling asleep, and he moved so slowly and stiffly that the warden cried to him:

"Hey, there! Quicker! Have you fallen asleep?"

Suddenly Yanson stopped.

"I don't want to be hanged," said he.

He was taken by the arms and led away, and began to stride obediently, raising his shoulders. Outside he found himself in the moist, spring air, and beads of sweat stood under his little nose. Notwithstanding that it was night, it was thawing very strongly and drops of water were dripping upon the stones. And waiting while the soldiers, clanking their sabres and bending their heads, were stepping into the unlighted black carriage, Yanson lazily moved his finger under his moist nose and adjusted the badly tied muffler about his neck.

CHAPTER IV

WE COME FROM ORYOL

THE same council-chamber of the military district court which had condemned Yanson had also condemned to death a peasant of the Government of Oryol, of the District of Yeletzk, Mikhail Golubets, nicknamed Tsiganok, also Tatarin. His latest crime, proven beyond question, had been the murder of three people and armed robbery. Behind that, his dark past disappeared in a depth of mystery. There were vague rumors that he had participated in a series of other murders and robberies, and in his path there was felt to be a dark trail of blood, fire, and drunken debauchery. He called himself murderer with utter frankness and sincerity, and scornfully regarded those who, according to the latest fashion, styled themselves "expropriators." Of his last crime, since it was useless for him to deny anything, he spoke freely and in detail, but in answer to questions about his past, he merely gritted his teeth, whistled, and said:

"Search for the wind of the fields!"

When he was annoyed in cross-examination, Tsiganok asumed a serious and dignified air:

"All of us from Oryol are thoroughbreds," he would say gravely and deliberately. "Oryol and Kroma are the homes of first-class thieves. Karachev and Livna are the breeding-places of thieves. And Yeletz—is the parent of all thieves. Now—what else is there to say?"

He was nicknamed Tsiganok (gypsy) because of his appearance and his thievish manner. He was black-haired, lean, with yellow spots on his prominent, Tartar-like cheek-bones. His glance was swift, brief, but fearfully direct and searching, and the thing upon which he looked for a moment seemed to lose something, seemed to deliver up to him a part of itself, and to become something else. It was just as unpleasant and repugnant to take a cigarette at which he looked, as though it had already been in his mouth. There was a certain constant restlessness in him, now twisting him like a rag, now throwing him about like a body of coiling live wires. And he drank water almost by the bucket.

To all questions during the trial he answered shortly, firmly, jumping up quickly, and at times he seemed to answer even with pleasure.

"Correct!" he would say.

Sometimes he emphasized it.

"Cor-r-rect!"

At one time, suddenly, when they were speaking of something that would hardly have seemed to suggest it, he jumped to his feet and asked the presiding judge:

"Will you allow me to whistle?"

"What for?" asked the judge, surprised.

"They said that I gave the signal to my comrades. I would like to show you how. It is very interesting."

The judge consented, somewhat wonderingly. Tsiganok quickly placed four fingers in his mouth, two fingers of each hand, rolled his eyes fiercely—and then the dead air of the courtroom was suddenly rent by a real, wild, murderer's whistle—at which frightened horses leap and rear on their hind legs and human faces involuntarily blanch. The mortal anguish of him who is to be assassinated, the wild joy of the murderer, the dreadful warning, the call, the gloom and loneliness of a stormy autumn night—all this rang in his piercing shriek, which was neither human nor beastly.

The presiding officer shouted — then waved his arm at Tsiganok, and Tsiganok obediently became silent. And, like an artist who had triumphantly performed a difficult aria, he sat down, wiped his wet fingers upon his coat, and surveyed those present with an air of satisfaction.

"What a robber!" said one of the judges, rubbing his ear.

Another one, however, with a wild Russian beard, but with the eyes of a Tartar, like those of Tsiganok, gazed pensively above Tsiganok's head, then smiled and remarked:

"It is indeed interesting."

With light hearts, without mercy, without the slightest pangs of conscience, the judges brought out against Tsiganok a verdict of death.

"Correct!" said Tsiganok, when the verdict was pronounced. "In the open field and on a cross-beam! Correct!"

And turning to the convoy, he hurled with bravado:

"Well, are we not going? Come on, you sour-coat. And hold your gun—I might take it away from you!"

The soldier looked at him sternly, with fear, exchanged glances with his comrade, and felt the lock of his gun. The other did the same. And all the way to the prison the soldiers felt that they were not walking but flying through the air—as if hypnotized by the prisoner, they felt neither the ground beneath their feet, nor the passage of time, nor themselves.

Mishka Tsiganok, like Yanson, had had

to spend seventeen days in prison before his execution. And all seventeen days passed as though they were one day—they were bound up in one inextinguishable thought of escape, of freedom, of life. The restlessness of Tsiganok, which was now repressed by the walls and the bars and the dead window through which nothing could be seen, turned all its fury upon himself and burned his soul like coals scattered upon boards. As though he were in a drunken vapor, bright but incomplete images swarmed upon him, failing and then becoming confused, and then again rushing through his mind in an unrestrainable blinding whirlwind—and all were bent toward escape, toward liberty, toward life. With his nostrils expanded, like those of a horse, Tsiganok smelt the air for hours long—it seemed to him that he could smell the odor of hemp, of the smoke of fire—the colorless and biting smell of burning. Now he whirled about in the room like a top, touching the walls, tapping them nervously with his fingers from time to time, taking aim, boring the ceiling with his gaze, filing the prison bars. By his restlessness, he had tired out the soldiers who watched him through the little window, and who, several times, in despair, had threatened to shoot. Tsiganok would retort, coarsely and derisively, and the quarrel would end peacefully because the dispute would soon turn into boorish, unoffending abuse, after which shooting would have seemed absurd and impossible.

Tsiganok slept during the nights soundly, without stirring, in unchanging yet live motionlessness, like a wire spring in temporary inactivity. But as soon as he arose, he immediately commenced to walk, to plan, to grope about. His hands were always dry and hot, but his heart at times would suddenly grow cold, as if a cake of unmelting ice had been placed upon his chest, sending a slight, dry shiver through his whole body. At such times, Tsiganok, always dark in complexion, would turn black, assuming the shade of bluish cast-iron. And he acquired a curious habit; as though he had eaten too much of something sickeningly sweet, he kept licking his lips, smacking them, and would spit on the floor, hissingly, through his teeth. When he spoke, he did not finish his words, so rapidly did his thoughts run that his tongue was unable to compass them.

One day the chief warden, accompanied by a soldier, entered his cell. He looked askance at the floor and said gruffly:

"Look! How dirty he has made it!"

Tsiganok retorted quickly:

"You've made the whole world dirty, you fat-face, and yet I haven't said anything to you. What brings you here?"

The warden, speaking as gruffly as before, asked him whether he would act as executioner. Tsiganok burst out laughing, showing his teeth.

"You can't find any one else? That's good! Go ahead, hang! Ha! ha! ha! The necks are there, the rope is there, but there is nobody to string it up. By God! that's good!"

"You'll save your neck if you do it."

"Of course—I couldn't hang them if I were dead. Well said, you fool!"

"Well, what do you say? Is it all the same to you?"

"And how do you hang them here? I suppose they're choked on the sly."

"No, with music," snarled the warden.

"Well, what a fool! Of course it can be done with music. This way!" and he began to sing, with a bold and daring swing.

"You have lost your wits, my friend," said the warden. "What do you say? Speak sensibly."

Tsiganok grinned.

"How eager you are! Come another time and I'll tell you."

After that, into that chaos of bright, yet incomplete images which oppressed Tsiganok by their impetuosity, a new image came —how good it would be to become a hangman in a red shirt. He pictured to himself vividly a square crowded with people, a high scaffold, and he, Tsiganok, in a red shirt walking about upon the scaffold with an ax. The sun shone overhead, gaily flashing from the ax, and everything was so gay and bright that even the man whose head was soon to be chopped off was smiling. And behind the crowd, wagons and the heads of horses could be seen—the peasants had come from the village; and beyond them, further, he could see the village itself.

"Ts-akh!"

Tsiganok smacked his lips, licking them, and spat. And suddenly he felt as though a fur cap had been pushed over his head to his very mouth—it became black and stifling, and his heart again became like a cake of unmelting ice, sending a slight, dry shiver through his whole body.

The warden came in twice again, and Tsiganok, showing his teeth, said:

"How eager you are! Come in again!"

Finally one day the warden shouted through the casement window as he passed rapidly:

"You've let your chance slip by, you fool! We've found somebody else."

"The devil take you! Hang yourself!" snarled Tsiganok, and he stopped dreaming of the execution.

But toward the end, the nearer he approached the time, the weight of the fragments of his broken images became unbearable. Tsiganok now felt like standing still, like spreading his legs and standing—but a whirling current of thoughts carried him away and there was nothing at which he could clutch—everything about him swam. And his sleep also became uneasy. Dreams even more violent than his thoughts appeared—new dreams, solid, heavy, like wooden painted blocks. And it was no longer like a current, but like an endless fall to an endless depth, a whirling flight through the whole visible world of colors.

When Tsiganok was free he had worn only a pair of dashing mustaches, but in the prison a short, black, bristly beard grew on his face and it made him look fearsome, insane. At times Tsiganok really lost his senses and whirled absurdly about in the cell, still tapping upon the rough, plastered walls nervously. And he drank water like a horse.

At times toward evening when they lit the lamp, Tsiganok would stand on all fours in the middle of his cell and would howl the quivering howl of a wolf. He was peculiarly serious while doing it, and would howl as though he were performing an important and indispensable act. He would fill his chest with air and then exhale it slowly in a prolonged tremulous howl, and, cocking his eyes, would listen intently as the sound issued forth. And the very quiver in his voice seemed in a manner intentional. He did not scream wildly, but drew out each note carefully in that mournful wail full of untold sorrow and terror.

Then he would suddenly break off howling and for several minutes would remain silent, still standing on all fours. Then suddenly he would mutter softly, staring at the ground:

"My darlings, my sweethearts! . . . My darlings, my sweethearts! have pity. . . . My darlings! . . . My sweethearts!"

And it seemed again as if he were listening intently to his own voice. As he said each word he would listen.

Then he would jump up and for a whole hour would curse continually.

He cursed picturesquely, shouting and rolling his blood-shot eyes.

"If you hang me—hang me!" and he would burst out cursing again.

And the sentinel, in the meantime white as chalk, weeping with pain and fright, would knock at the door with the butt-end of the gun and cry helplessly:

"I'll fire! I'll kill you as sure as I live! Do you hear?"

But he dared not shoot. If there was no actual rebellion they never fired at those who had been condemned to death. And Tsiganok would gnash his teeth, would curse and spit. His brain thus racked on a monstrously sharp blade between life and death was falling to pieces like a lump of dry clay.

When they entered the cell at midnight to lead Tsiganok to the execution he began to bustle about and seemed to have recovered his spirits. Again he had that sweet taste in his mouth, and his saliva collected abundantly, but his cheeks turned rosy and in his eyes began to glisten his former somewhat savage slyness. Dressing himself he asked the official:

"Who is going to do the hanging? A new man? I suppose he hasn't learned his job yet."

"You needn't worry about it," answered the official dryly.

"I can't help worrying, your Honor. I am going to be hanged, not you. At least don't be stingy with the government's soap on the noose."

"All right, all right! Keep quiet!"

"This man here has eaten all your soap," said Tsiganok, pointing to the warden. "See how his face shines."

"Silence!"

"Don't be stingy!"

And Tsiganok burst out laughing. But he began to feel that it was getting ever sweeter in his mouth, and suddenly his legs began to feel strangely numb. Still, on coming out into the yard, he managed to exclaim:

"The carriage of the Count of Bengal!"

CHAPTER V

KISS—AND SAY NOTHING

THE verdict concerning the five terrorists was pronounced finally and confirmed upon the same day. The condemned were not told when the execution would take place, but they knew from the usual procedure that they would be hanged the same night, or, at the very latest, upon the following night. And when it was proposed to them that they meet their relatives upon the following Thursday they understood that the execution would take place on Friday at dawn.

Tanya Kovalchuk had no near relatives, and those whom she had were somewhere in the wilderness in Little Russia and it was not likely that they even knew of the trial or of the coming execution. Musya and Werner, as unidentified people, were not supposed to have relatives, and only two, Sergey Golovin and Vasily Kashirin, were to meet their parents. Both of them looked upon that meeting with terror and anguish, yet they dared not refuse the old people the last word, the last kiss.

Sergey Golovin was particularly tortured by the thought of the coming meeting. He dearly loved his father and mother; he had seen them but a short while before, and now he was in a state of terror as to what would happen when they came to see him. The execution itself, in all its monstrous horror, in its brain-stunning madness, he could imagine more easily, and it seemed less terrible than these other few moments of meeting, brief and unsatisfactory, which seemed to reach beyond time, beyond life itself. How to look, what to think, what to say, his mind could not determine. The most simple and ordinary act, to take his father by the hand, to kiss him, and to say, "How do you do, father?" seemed to him unspeakably horrible in its monstrous, inhuman, absurd deceitfulness.

After the sentence the condemned were not placed together in one cell, as Tanya Kovalchuk had supposed they would be, but each was put in solitary confinement, and all the morning, until eleven o'clock, when his parents came, Sergey Golovin paced his cell furiously, tugged at his beard, frowned pitiably and muttered inaudibly. Sometimes he would stop abruptly, would breathe deeply and then exhale like a man who has been too long under water. But he was so healthy, his young life was so strong within him, that even in the moments of most painful suffering his blood played under his skin, reddening his cheeks, and his blue eyes shone brightly and frankly.

But everything was far different from what he had anticipated.

Nikolay Sergeyevich Golovin, Sergey's father, a retired colonel, was the first to enter the room where the meeting took place. He was all white—his face, his beard, his hair, and his hands—as if he were a snow statue attired in man's clothes. He had on the same old but well-cleaned coat, smelling of benzine, with new shoulder-straps crosswise, that he had always worn, and he entered firmly, with an air of stateliness, with strong and steady steps. He stretched out his white, thin hand and said loudly:

"How do you do, Sergey?"

Behind him Sergey's mother entered with short steps, smiling strangely. But she also pressed his hands and repeated loudly:

"How do you do, Seryozhenka?"

She kissed him on the lips and sat down silently. She did not rush over to him; she did not burst into tears; she did not break into a sob; she did not do any of the terrible things which Sergey had feared. She just kissed him and silently sat down. And with her trembling hands she even adjusted her black silk dress.

Sergey did not know that the colonel, having locked himself all the previous night in his little study, had deliberated upon this ritual with all his power. "We must not aggravate, but ease the last moments of our son," resolved the colonel firmly, and he carefully weighed every possible phase of the conversation, every act and movement that might take place on the following day. But somehow he became confused, forgetting what he had prepared, and he wept bitterly in the corner of the oilcloth-covered couch. In the morning he explained to his wife how she should behave at the meeting.

"The main thing is, kiss—and say nothing!" he taught her. "Later you may speak—after a while—but when you kiss him, be silent. Don't speak right after the kiss, do you understand? Or you will say what you should not say."

"I understand, Nikolay Sergeyevich," answered the mother, weeping.

"And you must not weep. For God's sake, do not weep! You will kill him if you weep, old woman!"

"Why do you weep?"

"With women one cannot help weeping. But you must not weep, do you hear?"

"Very well, Nikolay Sergeyevich."

Riding in the *drozhky,* he had intended to school her in the instructions again, but he forgot. And so they rode in silence, bent, both gray and old, and they were lost in thought, while the city was gay and noisy. It was Shrovetide, and the streets were crowded.

They sat down. Then the colonel stood up, assumed a studied pose, placing his right hand upon the border of his coat. Sergey sat for an instant, looked closely upon the wrinkled face of his mother and then jumped up.

"Be seated, Seryozhenka," begged the mother.

"Sit down, Sergey," repeated the father.

They became silent. The mother smiled.

"How we have petitioned for you, Seryozhenka! Father——"

"You should not have done that, mother——"

The colonel spoke firmly:

"We had to do it, Sergey, so that you should not think your parents had forsaken you."

They became silent again. It was terrible for them to utter even a word, as though each word in the language had lost its individual meaning and meant but one thing—Death. Sergey looked at his father's coat, which smelt of benzine, and thought: "They have no servant now, consequently he must have cleaned it himself. How is it that I never before noticed when he cleaned his coat? I suppose he does it in the morning." Suddenly he asked:

"And how is sister? Is she well?"

"Ninochka does not know anything," the mother answered hastily.

The colonel interrupted her sternly:

"Why should you tell a falsehood? The child read it in the newspapers. Let Sergey know that everybody—that those who are dearest to him—were thinking of him—at this time—and——"

He could not say any more and stopped. Suddenly the mother's face contracted, then it spread out, became agitated, wet and wild-looking. Her discolored eyes stared blindly, and her breathing became more frequent, and briefer, louder.

"Se — Se — Se—Ser ——" she repeated without moving her lips. "Ser——"

"Dear mother!"

The colonel strode forward, and all quivering in every fold of his coat, in every wrinkle of his face, not understanding how terrible he himself looked in his death-like whiteness, in his heroic, desperate firmness. He said to his wife:

"Be silent! Don't torture him! Don't torture him! He has to die! Don't torture him!"

Frightened, she had already become silent, but he still shook his clenched fists before him and repeated:

"Don't torture him!"

Then he stepped back, placed his trembling hands behind his back, and loudly, with an expression of forced calm, asked with pale lips:

"When?"

"To-morrow morning," answered Sergey, his lips also pale.

The mother looked at the ground, chewing her lips, as if she did not hear anything. And continuing to chew, she uttered these simple words, strangely, as though they dropped like lead:

"Ninochka told me to kiss you, Seryozhenka."

"Kiss her for me," said Sergey.

"Very well. The Khvostovs send you their regards."

"Which Khvostovs? Oh, yes!"

The colonel interrupted:

"Well, we must go. Get up, mother; we must go." The two men lifted the weakened old woman.

"Bid him good-by!" ordered the colonel. "Make the sign of the cross."

She did everything as she was told. But as she made the sign of the cross, and kissed her son a brief kiss, she shook her head and murmured weakly:

"No, it isn't the right way! It is not the right way! What will I say? How will I say it? No, it is not the right way!"

"Good-by, Sergey!" said the father. They shook hands, and kissed each other quickly but heartily.

"You——" began Sergey.

"Well?" asked the father abruptly.

"No, no! It is not the right way! How shall I say it?" repeated the mother weakly, nodding her head. She had sat down again and was rocking herself back and forth.

"You——" Sergey began again. Suddenly his face wrinkled pitiably, childishly, and his eyes filled with tears immediately. Through the sparkling gleams of his tears he looked closely into the white face of his father, whose eyes had also filled.

"You, father, are a noble man!"

"What is that? What are you saying?" said the colonel, surprised. And then suddenly, as if broken in two, he fell with his head upon his son's shoulder. He had been taller than Sergey, but now he became short, and his dry, downy head lay like a white ball upon his son's shoulder. And they kissed silently and passionately: Sergey kissed the silvery white hair, and the old man kissed the prisoner's garb.

"And I?" suddenly said a loud voice.

They looked around. Sergey's mother

was standing, her head thrown back, looking at them angrily, almost with contempt.

"What is it, mother?" cried the colonel.

"And I?" she said, shaking her head with insane intensity. "You kiss—and I? You men! Yes? And I? And I?"

"Mother!" Sergey rushed over to her.

What took place then it is unnecessary and impossible to describe. . . .

The last words of the colonel were:

"I give you my blessing for your death, Seryozha. Die bravely, like an officer."

And they went away. Somehow they went away. They had been there, they had stood, they had spoken—and suddenly they had gone. Here sat his mother, there stood his father—and suddenly somehow they had gone away. Returning to the cell, Sergey lay down on the cot, his face turned toward the wall, in order to hide it from the soldiers, and he wept for a long time. Then, exhausted by his tears, he slept soundly.

To Vasily Kashirin only his mother came. His father, who was a wealthy tradesman, did not want to come. Vasily met the old woman, as he was pacing up and down the room, trembling with cold, although it was warm, even hot. And the conversation was brief, painful.

"It wasn't worth coming, mother. You'll only torture yourself and me."

"Why did you do it, Vasya? Why did you do it? Oh, Lord!" The old woman burst out weeping, wiping her face with the ends of her black, woolen kerchief. And with the habit which he and his brothers had always had of crying at their mother, who did not understand anything, he stopped, and, shuddering as with cold, spoke angrily:

"There! You see! I knew it! You understand nothing, mother! Nothing!"

"Well—well—all right! Do you feel—cold?"

"Cold!" Vasily answered bluntly, and again began to pace the room, looking at his mother askance, as if annoyed.

"Perhaps you have caught cold?"

"Oh, mother what is a cold, when——" and he waved his hand helplessly.

The old woman was about to say: "And your father ordered wheat cakes beginning with Monday," but she was frightened, and said:

"I told him: 'It is your son, you should go, give him your blessing.' No, the old beast persisted——"

"Let him go to the devil! What sort of father has he been to me? He has been a scoundrel all his life, and remains a scoundrel!"

"Vasenka! Do you speak of your father like this?" said the old woman reproachfully, straightening herself.

"About my father!"

"About your own father?"

"He is no father to me!"

It was strange and absurd. Before him was the thought of death, while here something small, empty and trivial arose, and his words cracked like the shells of nuts under foot. And almost crying with sorrow—because of the eternal misunderstanding which all his life long had stood like a wall between him and those nearest to him, and which even now, in the last hour before death, peered at him stupidly and strangely through small, widely opened eyes—Vasily exclaimed:

"Don't you understand that I am to be hanged soon? Hanged! Do you understand it? Hanged!"

"You shouldn't have harmed anybody and nobody would——" cried the old woman.

"My God! What is this? Even beasts do not act like this! Am I not your son?"

He began to cry, and seated himself in a corner. The old woman also burst out crying in her corner. Powerless, even for an instant, to blend in a feeling of love and to offset by it the horror of impending death, they wept their cold tears of loneliness which did not warm their hearts. The mother said:

"You ask whether I am a mother to you? You reproach me! And I have grown completely gray during these days. I have become an old woman. And yet you say—you reproach me!"

"Well, mother, it is all right. Forgive

me. It is time for you to go. Kiss my brothers for me."

"Am I not your mother? Do I not feel sorry?"

At last she went away. She wept bitterly, wiping her face with the edges of her kerchief, and she did not see the road. And the farther she got from the prison the more bitterly she wept. She retraced her steps to the prison, and then she strangely lost her way in the city in which she had been born, in which she lived to her old age. She strolled into a deserted little garden with a few old, gnarled trees, and she seated herself upon a wet bench, from which the snow had melted. And suddenly she understood. He was to be hanged upon the morrow!

The old woman jumped up, about to run, but suddenly her head began to swim terribly and she fell to the ground. The icy path was wet and slippery, and she could not rise. She turned about, lifted herself on her elbows and knelt, then fell back on her side. The black kerchief had slipped down, baring upon the back of her head a bald spot amid her muddy-gray hair; and then somehow it seemed to her that she was feasting at a wedding, that her son was getting married, and she had been drinking wine and had become intoxicated.

"I can't! My God! I can't!" she cried, as though declining something. Swaying her head, she crawled over the wet, frozen crust, and all the time it seemed to her that they were pouring out more wine for her, more wine!

And her heart had already begun to pain her from her intoxicated laughter, from the rejoicing, from the wild dancing—and they kept on pouring more wine for her—pouring more wine!

CHAPTER VI

THE HOURS ARE RUSHING

ON the fortress where the condemned terrorists were imprisoned there was a steeple with an old-fashioned clock upon it. At every hour, at every half-hour, and at every quarter-hour the clock rang out in long-drawn, mournful chimes, slowly melting high in the air, like the distant and plaintive call of migrating birds. In the daytime, this strange and sad music was lost in the noise of the city, of the wide and crowded street which passed near the fortress. The cars buzzed along, the hoofs of the horses beat upon the pavements, the rocking automobiles honked in the distance, peasant *izvozchiks* had come especially from the outskirts of the city for the Shrovetide season and the tinkling of the bells upon the necks of their little horses filled the air. The prattle of voices—an intoxicated, merry Shrovetide prattle of voices arose everywhere. And in the midst of these various noises there was the young thawing spring, the muddy pools on the meadows, the trees of the squares which had suddenly become black. From the sea a warm breeze was blowing in broad, moist gusts. It was almost as if one could have seen the tiny fresh particles of air carried away, merged into the free, endless expanse of the atmosphere—could have heard them laughing in their flight.

At night the street grew quiet in the lonely light of the large, electric sun. And then, the enormous fortress, within whose walls there was not a single light, passed into darkness and silence, separating itself from the ever living, stirring city by a wall of silence, motionlessness and darkness. Then it was that the strokes of the clock became audible. A strange melody, foreign to earth, was slowly and mournfully born and died out up in the heights. It was born again; deceiving the ear, it rang plaintively and softly—it broke off—and rang again. Like large, transparent, glassy drops, hours and minutes descended from an unknown height into a metallic, softly resounding bell.

This was the only sound that reached the cells, by day and night, where the condemned remained in solitary confinement. Through the roof, through the thickness of the stone walls, it penetrated, stirring the silence—it passed unnoticed, to return again, also unnoticed. Sometimes they awaited it in despair, living from one sound to the next, trusting the silence no longer. Only important criminals were sent to this prison. There were special rules there, stern, grim and severe, like the corner of the fortress wall, and if there be nobility in cruelty, then the dull, dead, solemnly mute silence, which caught the slightest rustle and breathing, was noble.

And in this solemn silence, broken by the mournful tolling of the departing minutes, separated from all that lives, five human beings, two women and three men, waited for the advent of night, of dawn and the execution, and all of them prepared for it, each in his or her own way.

CHAPTER VII

THERE IS NO DEATH

JUST as Tanya Kovalchuk had thought all her life only of others and never of herself, so now she suffered and grieved painfully, but only for her comrades. She pictured death, only as awaiting them, as something tormenting only to Sergey Golovin, to Musya, to the others—as for herself, it did not concern her.

As a recompense for her firmness and restraint in the courtroom she wept for long hours, as old women who have experienced great misery, or as very sympathetic and kind-hearted young people know how to weep. And the fear that perhaps Seryozha was without tobacco or Werner without the strong tea to which he was accustomed, in addition to the fact that they were to die, caused her no less pain than the idea of the execution itself. Death was something inevitable and even unimportant, of which it was not worth while to think; but for a man in prison, before his execution, to be left without tobacco—that was altogether unbearable. She recalled and went over in her mind all the pleasant details of their life together, and then she grew faint with fear when she pictured to herself the meeting between Sergey and his parents.

She felt particularly sorry for Musya. It had long seemed to her that Musya loved Werner, and although this was not a fact, she still dreamed of something good and bright for both of them. When she had been free, Musya had worn a silver ring, on which was the design of a skull, bones, and a crown of thorns about them. Tanya Kovalchuk had often looked upon the ring as a symbol of doom, and she would ask Musya, now in jest, now in earnest, to remove the ring.

"Make me a present of it," she had begged.

"No, Tanechka, I will not give it to you.

But perhaps you will soon have another ring upon your finger."

For some reason or other they all in turn had thought that she would doubtless soon marry, and this had offended her—she wanted no husband. And recalling these half-jesting conversations with Musya, and the fact that now Musya was actually condemned to death, she choked with tears in her maternal pity. And each time the clock struck she raised her tear-stained face and listened—how were they in the other cells receiving this drawn-out, persistent call of death?

But Musya was happy.

With her hands folded behind her back, dressed in a prisoner's garb which was much too large for her, and which made her look very much like a man—like a stripling dressed in some one else's clothes—she paced her cell evenly and tirelessly. The sleeves of the coat were too long for her, and she turned them up, and her thin, almost childish, emaciated hands peeped out of the wide holes like a beautiful flower out of a coarse earthen jug. The rough material of the coat rubbed her thin white neck, and sometimes Musya would free her throat with both hands and would cautiously feel the spot where the irritated skin was red and smarted.

Musya paced the cell, and, blushing in agitation, she imagined that she was justifying herself before the people. She tried to justify herself for the fact that she, who was so young, so insignificant, who had done so little, and who was not at all a heroine, was yet to undergo the same honorable and beautiful death by which real heroes and martyrs had died before her. With unshakable faith in human kindness, in their compassion, in their love, she pictured to herself how people were now agitated on her account, how they suffered, how they pitied her, and she felt so ashamed that she blushed, as if, by dying upon the scaffold, she had committed some tremendous, awkward blunder.

At the last meeting with their counsel she had asked him to bring her poison, but suddenly she had changed her mind. What if he and the others, she thought, should consider that she was doing it merely to become conspicuous, or out of cowardice, that instead of dying modestly and unnoticed, she was attempting to glorify herself. And she added hastily:

"No, it isn't necessary."

And now she desired but one thing—to be able to explain to people, to prove to them so that they should have not the slightest doubt that she was not at all a heroine, that it was not terrible to die, that they should not feel sorry for her, nor trouble themselves about her. She wished to be able to explain to them that she was not at all to blame that she, who was so young and so insignificant, was to undergo such a martyr's death, and that so much trouble should be made on her account.

Like a person who is actually accused of a crime, Musya sought justification. She endeavored to find something that would at least make her sacrifice more momentous, which might give it real value. She reasoned:

"Of course, I am young and could have lived for a long time. But——"

And as a candle darkens in the glare of the rising sun, so her youth and her life seemed dull and dark compared to that great and resplendent radiance which would shine above her simple head. There was no justification.

But perhaps that peculiar something which she bore in her soul—boundless love, boundless eagerness to do great deeds, her boundless contempt for herself—was a justification in itself. She felt that she was really not to blame that she was hindered from doing the things she could have done, which she had wished to do—that she had been smitten upon the threshold of the temple, at the foot of the altar.

But if that were so, if a person is appreciated not only for what he has done, but also for what he had intended to do—then—then she was worthy of the crown of the martyr!

"Is it possible?" thought Musya bashfully. "Is it possible that I am worthy of it? That I deserve that people should weep for me, should be agitated over my fate, over such a little and insignificant girl?"

And she was seized with sudden joy. There were no doubts, no hesitations—she was received into their midst—she entered justified the ranks of those noble people who always ascend to heaven through fires, tortures and executions. Bright peace and tranquillity and endless, calmly radiant happiness! It was as if she had already departed from earth and was nearing the unknown sun of truth and life, and was incorporeally soaring in its light.

"And that is—Death? That is not Death!" thought Musya blissfully.

And if scientists, philosophers and hangmen from the world over should come to her cell, spreading before her books, scalpels, axes and nooses, and were to attempt to prove to her that Death existed, that a human being dies and is killed, that there is no immortality, they would only surprise her. How could there be no deathlessness, since she was already deathless? Of what other deathlessness, of what other death, could there be a question, since she was already dead and immortal, alive in death, as she had been dead in life?

And if a coffin were brought into her cell with her own decomposing body in it, and she were told:

"Look! That is you!"

She would look and would answer:

"No, it is not I."

And if they should attempt to convince her, frightening her by the ominous sight of her own decomposed body, that it was she —she, Musya, would answer with a smile:

"No. You think that it is I, but it isn't. I am the one you are speaking to; how can I be the other one?"

"But you will die and become like that."

"No, I will not die."

"You will be executed. Here is the noose."

"I will be executed, but I will not die. How can I die, when I am already—now—immortal?"

And the scientists and philosophers and

hangmen would retreat, speaking with a shudder:

"Do not touch this place. It is holy."

What else was Musya thinking about? She was thinking of many things, for to her the thread of life was not broken by Death, but kept winding along calmly and evenly. She thought of her comrades, of those who were far away, and who in pain and sorrow were living through the execution together with them, and of those near by who were to mount the scaffold with her. She was surprised at Vasily—that he should have been so disturbed—he, who had always been so brave, and who had jested with Death. Thus, only on Tuesday morning, when all together they had attached explosive projectiles to their belts, which several hours later were to tear them into pieces, Tanya Kovalchuk's hands had trembled with nervousness, and it had become necessary to put her aside, while Vasily jested, made merry, turned about, and was even so reckless that Werner had said sternly:

"You must not be too familiar with Death."

What was he afraid of now? But this incomprehensible fear was so foreign to Musya's soul that she ceased searching for the cause of it—and suddenly she was seized with a desperate desire to see Seryozha Golovin, to laugh with him. She meditated a little while, and then an even more desperate desire came over her to see Werner and to convince him of something. And imagining to herself that Werner was in the next cell, driving his heels into the ground with his distinct, measured steps, Musya spoke, as if addressing him:

"No, Werner, my dear; it is all nonsense; it isn't at all important whether or not you are killed. You are a sensible man, but you seem to be playing chess, and that by taking one figure after another the game is won. The important thing, Werner, is that we ourselves are ready to die. Do you understand? What do those people think? That there is nothing more terrible than death. They themselves have invented Death, they are themselves afraid of it, and they try to frighten us with it. I should like to do this—I should like to go out alone before a whole regiment of soldiers and fire upon them with a revolver. It would not matter that I would be alone, while they would be thousands, or that I might not kill any of them. It is that which is important—that they are thousands. When thousands kill one, it means that the one has conquered. That is true, Werner, my dear. . . ."

But this, too, became so clear to her that she did not feel like arguing further—Werner must understand it himself. Perhaps her mind simply did not want to stop at one thought—just as a bird that soars with ease, which sees endless horizons, and to which all space, all the depth, all the joy of the soft and caressing azure are accessible. The bell of the clock rang unceasingly, disturbing the deep silence. And into this harmonious, remote, beautiful sound the thoughts of the people flowed, and also began to ring for her; and the smoothly gliding images turned into music. It was just as if, on a quiet, dark night, Musya was riding along a broad, even road, while the easy springs of the carriage rocked her and the little bells tinkled. All alarm and agitation had passed, the fatigued body had dissolved in the darkness, and her joyously wearied fancy calmly created bright images, carried away by their color and their peaceful tranquillity. Musya recalled three of her comrades who had been hanged but a short time before, and their faces seemed bright and happy and near to her—nearer than those in life. Thus does a man think with joy in the morning of the house of his friends where he is to go in the evening, and a greeting rises to his smiling lips.

Musya became very tired from walking. She lay down cautiously on the cot and continued to dream with slightly closed eyes. The clock-bell rang unceasingly, stirring the mute silence, and bright, singing images floated calmly before her. Musya thought:

"Is it possible that this is Death? My God! How beautiful it is! Or is it Life?

I do not know. I do not know. I will look and listen."

Her hearing had long given way to her imagination—from the first moment of her imprisonment. Inclined to be very musical, her ear had become keen in the silence, and on this background of silence, out of the meagre bits of reality, the footsteps of the guards in the corridors, the ringing of the clock, the rustling of the wind on the iron roof, the creaking of the lantern—it created complete musical pictures. At first Musya was afraid of them, brushed them away from her as if they were the hallucinations of a sickly mind. But later she understood that she herself was well, and that this was no derangement of any kind—and she gave herself up to the dreams calmly.

And now, suddenly, she seemed to hear clearly and distinctly the sounds of military music. In astonishment, she opened her eyes, lifted her head—outside the window was black night, and the clock was striking. "Again," she thought calmly, and closed her eyes. And as soon as she did so the music resounded anew. She could hear distinctly how the soldiers, a whole regiment, were coming from behind the corner of the fortress, on the right, and now they were passing her window. Their feet beat time with measured steps upon the frozen ground: One-two! One-two! She could even hear at times the leather of the boots creaking, how suddenly some one's foot slipped and immediately recovered its steps. And the music came ever nearer—it was an entirely unfamiliar but a very loud and spirited holiday march. Evidently there was some sort of celebration in the fortress.

Now the band came up alongside of her window and the cell was filled with merry, rhythmic, harmoniously blended sounds. One large brass trumpet brayed harshly out of tune, now too late, now comically running ahead—Musya could almost see the little soldier playing it, a great expression of earnestness on his face—and she laughed.

Then everything moved away. The footsteps died out—One-two! One-two! At a distance the music sounded still more beautiful and cheerful. The trumpet resounded now and then with its merry, loud brass voice, out of tune,—and then everything died away. And the clock on the tower struck again, slowly, mournfully, hardly stirring the silence.

"They are gone!" thought Musya, with a feeling of slight sadness. She felt sorry for the departing sounds, which had been so cheerful and so comical. She was even sorry for the departed little soldiers, because those busy soldiers, with their brass trumpets and their creaking boots, were of an entirely different sort, not at all like those at whom she had felt like firing a revolver.

"Come again!" she begged tenderly. And more came. The figures bent over her, they surrounded her in a transparent cloud and lifted her up, where the migrating birds were soaring and screaming, like heralds. On the right of her, on the left, above and below her—they screamed like heralds. They called, they announced from afar their flight. They flapped their wide wings and the darkness supported them, even as the light had supported them. And on their convex breasts, cleaving the air asunder, the city far below reflected a blue light. Musya's heart beat ever more evenly, her breathing grew ever more calm and quiet. She was falling asleep. Her face looked fatigued and pale. Beneath her eyes were dark circles, her girlish, emaciated hands seemed so thin,—but upon her lips was a smile. To-morrow, with the rise of the sun, this human face would be distorted with an inhuman grimace, her brain would be covered with thick blood, and her eyes would bulge from their sockets and look glassy,—but now she slept quietly and smiled in her great immortality.

Musya fell asleep.

And the life of the prison went on, deaf and sensitive, blind and sharp-sighted, like eternal alarm itself. Somewhere people were walking. Somewhere people were whispering. A gun clanked. It seemed as if some one shouted. Perhaps no one shouted at all—perhaps it merely seemed so in the silence.

The little casement window in the door

opened noiselessly. A dark, mustached face appeared in the black hole. For a long time it stared at Musya in astonishment—and then disappeared as noiselessly as it had appeared.

The bells rang and sang, for a long time, painfully. It seemed as if the tired Hours were climbing up a high mountain toward midnight, and that it was becoming ever harder and harder to ascend. They fall, they slip, they slide down with a groan—and then again, they climb painfully toward the black height.

Somewhere people were walking. Somewhere people were whispering. And they were already harnessing the horses to the black carriages without lanterns.

CHAPTER VIII

THERE IS DEATH AS WELL AS LIFE

Sergey Golovin never thought of death, as though it were something not to be considered, something that did not concern him in the least. He was a strong, healthy, cheerful youth, endowed with that calm, clear joy of living which causes every evil thought and feeling that might injure life to disappear from the organism without leaving any trace. Just as all cuts, wounds and stings on his body healed rapidly, so all that weighed upon his soul and wounded it immediately rose to the surface and disappeared. And he brought into every work, even into his enjoyments, the same calm and optimistic seriousness,—it mattered not whether he was occupied with photography, with bicycling or with preparations for a terroristic act. Everything in life was joyous, everything in life was important, everything should be done well.

And he did everything well: he was an excellent sailor, an expert shot with the revolver. He was as faithful in friendship as in love, and a fanatic believer in the "word of honor." His comrades laughed at him, saying that if the most notorious spy told him upon his word of honor that he was not a spy, Sergey would believe him and would shake hands with him as with any comrade. He had one fault,—he was convinced that he could sing well, whereas in fact he had no ear for music and even sang the revolutionary songs out of tune, and felt offended when his friends laughed at him.

"Either you are all asses, or I am an ass," he would declare seriously and even angrily. And all his friends as seriously declared: "You are an ass. We can tell by your voice."

But, as is sometimes the case with good people, he was perhaps liked more for this little foible than for his good qualities.

He feared death so little and thought of it so little that on the fatal morning, before leaving the house of Tanya Kovalchuk, he was the only one who had breakfasted properly, with an appetite. He drank two glasses of tea with milk, and a whole five-copeck roll of bread. Then he glanced at Werner's untouched bread and said:

"Why don't you eat? Eat. We must brace up."

"I don't feel like eating."

"Then I'll eat it. May I?"

"You have a fine appetite, Seryozha."

Instead of answering, Sergey, his mouth full, began to sing in a dull voice, out of tune:

"Hostile whirlwinds are blowing over us . . ."

After the arrest he at first grew sad; the work had not been done well, they had failed; but then he thought: "There is something else now that must be done well—and that is, to die," and he cheered up again. And however strange it may seem, beginning with the second morning in the fortress, he commenced devoting himself to gymnastics according to the unusually rational system of a certain German named Müller, which absorbed his interest. He undressed himself completely and, to the alarm and astonishment of the guard who watched him, he carefully went through all the prescribed eighteen exercises. The fact that the guard watched him and was apparently astonished, pleased him as a propagandist of the Müller system; and although he knew that he would get no answer he nevertheless spoke to the eye staring in the little window:

"It's a good system, my friend, it braces you up. It should be introduced in your regiment," he shouted convincingly and kindly, so as not to frighten the soldier, not suspecting that the guard considered him a harmless lunatic.

The fear of death came over him gradually. It was as if somebody were striking his heart a powerful blow with the fist from below. This sensation was rather painful than terrible. Then the sensation was forgotten, but it returned again a few hours later, and each time it grew more intense and of longer duration, and thus it began to assume vague outlines of some great, even unbearable fear.

"Is it possible that I am afraid?" thought Sergey in astonishment. "What nonsense!"

It was not he who was afraid,—it was his young, sound, strong body, which could not be deceived either by the exercises prescribed by the Müller system, or by the cold rub-downs. On the contrary, the stronger and the fresher his body became after the cold water, the keener and the more unbearable became the sensations of his recurrent fear. And just at those moments when, during his freedom, he had felt a special influx of the joy and power of life,—in the mornings after he had slept soundly and gone through his physical exercises,—now there appeared this deadening fear which was so foreign to his nature. He noticed this and thought:

"It is foolish, Sergey! To die more easily, you should weaken the body and not strengthen it. It is foolish!"

So he dropped his gymnastics and the rub-downs. To the soldier he shouted, as if to explain and justify himself:

"Never mind that I have stopped. It's a good thing, my friend,—but not for those who are to be hanged. But it's very good for all others."

And, indeed, he began to feel somewhat better. He tried also to eat less, so as to grow still weaker, but notwithstanding the lack of pure air and exercises, his appetite was very good,—it was difficult for him to control it, and he ate everything that was brought to him. Then he began to manage differently—before starting to eat he would pour out half into the pail, and this seemed to work. A dull drowsiness and faintness came over him.

"I'll show you what I can do!" he threatened his body, and at the same time sadly, yet tenderly he felt his flabby, softened muscles with his hand.

Soon, however, his body grew accustomed to this régime as well, and the fear of death appeared again—not so keen, nor so burning, but more disgusting, somewhat akin to a nauseating sensation. "It's because they are dragging it out so long," thought Sergey. "It would be a good idea to sleep all the time till the day of the execution," and he tried to sleep as much as possible. At first he succeeded, but later, either because he had slept too much, or for some other reason, insomnia appeared. And with it came eager, penetrating thoughts and a longing for life.

"I am not afraid of this devil!" he thought of Death. "I simply feel sorry for my life. It is a splendid thing, no matter what the pessimists say about it. What if they were to hang a pessimist? Ah, I feel sorry for life, very sorry! And why does my beard grow now? It didn't grow before, but suddenly it grows—why?"

He shook his head mournfully, heaving long, painful sighs. Silence—then a sigh; then a brief silence again—followed by a longer, deeper sigh.

Thus it went on until the trial and the terrible meeting with his parents. When he awoke in his cell the next day he realized clearly that everything between him and life was ended, that there were only a few empty hours of waiting and then death would come, —and a strange sensation took possession of him. He felt as though he had been stripped, stripped entirely,—as if not only his clothes, but the sun, the air, the noise of voices and his ability to do things had been wrested from him. Death was not there as yet, but life was there no longer,—there was something new, something astonishing, inexplicable, not entirely reasonable and yet not altogether without meaning,—something so deep and mysterious and supernatural that it was impossible to understand.

"Fie, you devil!" wondered Sergey, painfully. "What is this? Where am I? I—who am I?"

He examined himself attentively, with interest, beginning with his large prison slippers, ending with his stomach where his coat protruded. He paced the cell, spreading out his arms and continuing to survey himself like a woman in a new dress which is too long for her. He tried to turn his head, and it turned. And this strange, terrible, uncouth creature was he, Sergey Golovin, and soon he would be no more!

Everything became strange.

He tried to walk across the cell—and it seemed strange to him that he could walk. He tried to sit down—and it seemed strange to him that he could sit. He tried to drink some water—and it seemed strange to him that he could drink, that he could swallow, that he could hold the cup, that he had fingers and that those fingers were trembling. He choked, began to cough and while coughing, thought: "How strange it is that I am coughing."

"Am I losing my reason?" thought Sergey, growing cold. "Am I coming to that, too? The devil take them!"

He rubbed his forehead with his hand, and this also seemed strange to him. And then he remained breathless, motionless, petrified for hours, suppressing every thought, all loud breathing, all motion,—for every thought seemed to him but madness, every motion—madness. Time was no more; it appeared transformed into space, airless and transparent, into an enormous square upon which all were there—the earth and life and people. He saw all that at one glance, all to the very end, to the mysterious abyss—Death. And he was tortured not by the fact that Death was visible, but that both Life and Death were visible at the same time. The curtain which through eternity has hidden the mystery of life and the mystery of death was pushed aside by a sacrilegious hand, and the mysteries ceased to be mysteries—yet they remained incomprehensible, like the Truth written in a foreign tongue. There were no conceptions in his human mind, no words in his human language that could define what he saw. And the words "I am afraid" were uttered by him only because there were no other words, because no other conceptions existed, nor could other conceptions exist which would grasp this new, unhuman condition. Thus would it be with a man if, while remaining within the bounds of human reason, experience and feelings, he were suddenly to see God Himself. He would see Him but would not understand, even though he knew that it was God, and he would tremble with inconceivable sufferings of incomprehension.

"There is Müller for you!" he suddenly uttered loudly, with extreme conviction, and shook his head. And with that unexpected break in his feelings, of which the human soul is so capable, he laughed heartily and cheerfully.

"Oh, Müller! My dear Müller! Oh, you splendid German! After all you are right, Müller, and I am an ass!"

He paced the cell quickly several times and to the great astonishment of the soldier who was watching him through the peep-hole, he quickly undressed himself and cheerfully went through all the eighteen exercises with the greatest care. He stretched and expanded his young, somewhat emaciated body, sat down for a moment, drew deep breaths of air and exhaled it, stood up on tip-toe, stretched his arms and his feet. And after each exercise he announced, with satisfaction:

"That's it! That's the real way, Müller!" His cheeks flushed; drops of warm, pleasant perspiration came from the pores of his body, and his heart beat soundly and evenly.

"The fact is, Müller," philosophized Sergey, expanding his chest so that the ribs under his thin, tight skin were outlined clearly,—"the fact is, that there is a nineteenth exercise—to hang by the neck motionless. That is called execution. Do you understand, Müller? They take a live man, let us say Sergey Golovin, they swaddle him as a doll and they hang him by the neck until he is dead. It is a foolish exercise, Müller, but it can't be helped,—we have to do it."

He bent over on the right side and repeated:

"We have to do it, Müller."

CHAPTER IX

DREADFUL SOLITUDE

UNDER the same ringing of the clock, separated from Sergey and Musya by only a few empty cells, but yet so painfully desolate and alone in the whole world as though no other soul existed, poor Vasily Kashirin was passing the last hours of his life in terror and in anguish.

Perspiring, his moist shirt clinging to his body, his once curly hair disheveled, he tossed about in the cell convulsively and hopelessly, like a man suffering from an unbearable physical torture. He would sit down for awhile, then start to run again, he would press his forehead against the wall, stop and seek something with his eyes—as if looking for some medicine. His expression changed as though he had two different faces. The former, the young face, had disappeared somewhere, and a new one, a terrible face that had seemed to have come out of the darkness, had taken its place.

The fear of death had come upon him all at once and taken possession of him completely and forcibly. In the morning, while facing almost certain death, he had been care-free and had scorned it, but toward evening when he was placed in a cell in solitary confinement, he was whirled and carried away by a wave of mad fear. So long as he went of his own free will to face danger and death, so long as he had death, even though it seemed terrible, in his own hands, he felt at ease. He was even cheerful; in the sensation of boundless freedom, of brave and firm conviction of his fearless will, his little, shrunken, womanish fear was drowned, leaving no trace. With an infernal machine at his girdle, he made the cruel force of dynamite his own, also its fiery death-bearing power. And as he walked along the street, amidst the bustling, plain people, who were occupied with their affairs, who were hurriedly avoiding the dangers from the horses of carriages and cars, he seemed to himself as a stranger from another, unknown world, where neither death nor fear was known.

And suddenly this harsh, wild, stupefying change. He can no longer go where he pleases, but he is led where others please. He can no longer choose the place he likes, but he is placed in a stone cage, and locked up like a thing. He can no longer choose freely, like all people, between life and death, but he will surely and inevitably be put to death. The incarnation of will-power, life and strength an instant before, he has now become a wretched image of the most pitiful weakness in the world. He has been transformed into an animal waiting to be slaughtered, a deaf-mute object which may be taken from place to place, burnt and broken. It matters not what he might say, nobody would listen to his words, and if he endeavored to shout, they would stop his mouth with a rag. Whether he can walk alone or not, they will take him away and hang him.

And if he should offer resistance, struggle or lie down on the ground—they will overpower him, lift him, bind him and carry him, bound, to the gallows. And the fact that this machine-like work will be performed over him by human beings like himself, lent to them a new, extraordinary and ominous aspect—they seemed to him like ghosts that came to him for this one purpose, or like automatic puppets on springs. They would seize him, take him, carry him, hang him, pull him by the feet. They would cut the rope, take him down, carry him off and bury him.

From the first day of his imprisonment the people and life seemed to him to have turned into an incomprehensibly terrible world of phantoms and automatic puppets. Almost maddened with fear, he attempted to picture to himself that human beings had tongues and that they could speak, but he could not—they seemed to him to be mute. He tried to recall their speech, the meaning of the words that people used in their relations with one another—but he could not. Their mouths seemed to open, some sounds were heard; then they moved their feet and disappeared. And nothing more.

Thus would a man feel if he were at night alone in his house and suddenly all objects were to come to life, start to move and overpower him. And suddenly they would all begin to judge him: the cupboard, the chair, the writing-table and the divan. He would cry and toss about, entreating, calling for help, while they would speak among themselves in their own language, and then would lead him to the scaffold,—they, the cupboard, the chair, the writing-table and the divan. And the other objects would look on.

To Vasily Kashirin, who was condemned to death by hanging, everything now seemed like children's playthings: his cell, the door with the peephole, the strokes of the wound-up clock, the carefully molded fortress, and especially that mechanical puppet with the gun who stamped his feet in the corridor, and the others who, frightening him, peeped into his cell through the little window and handed him the food in silence. And that which he was experiencing was not the fear of death;

death was now rather welcome to him. Death with all its eternal mysteriousness and incomprehensibility was more acceptable to his reason than this strangely and fantastically changed world. What is more, death seemed to have been destroyed completely in this insane world of phantoms and puppets, having lost its great and enigmatic significance, becoming something mechanical and only for that reason terrible. He would be seized, taken, led, hanged, pulled by the feet, the rope would be cut, he would be taken down, carried off and buried.

And the man would have disappeared from the world.

At the trial the nearness of his comrades brought Kashirin to himself. For an instant he imagined he saw real people; they were sitting and trying him, speaking like human beings, listening, apparently understanding him. But as he mentally rehearsed the meeting with his mother he clearly felt with the terror of a man who is beginning to lose his reason and who realizes it, that this old woman in the black little kerchief was only an artificial, mechanical puppet, of the kind that can say "pa-pa," "ma-ma," but somewhat better constructed. He tried to speak to her, while thinking at the same time with a shudder:

"O Lord! That is a puppet. A mother doll. And there is a soldier-puppet, and there, at home, is a father-puppet, and this is the puppet of Vasily Kashirin."

It seemed to him that in another moment he would hear somewhere the creaking of the mechanism, the screeching of unoiled wheels. When his mother began to cry, something human again flashed for an instant, but at the very first words it disappeared again, and it was interesting and terrible to see that water was flowing from the eyes of the doll.

Then, in his cell, when the terror had become unbearable, Vasily Kashirin attempted to pray. Of all that had surrounded his childhood days in his father's house under the guise of religion only a repulsive, bitter and irritating sediment remained; but faith there was none. But once, perhaps in his earliest childhood, he had heard a few words which had filled him with palpitating emotion and which remained during all his life enwrapped with tender poetry. These words were:

"The joy of all the afflicted . . ."

It had happened, during painful periods in his life, that he whispered to himself, not in prayer, without being definitely conscious of it, these words: "The joy of all the afflicted"—and suddenly he would feel relieved and a desire would come over him to go to some dear friend and question gently:

"Our life—is this life? Eh, my dearest, is this life?"

And then suddenly it would appear laughable to him and he would feel like mussing up his hair, putting forth his knee and thrusting out his chest as though to receive heavy blows; saying: "Here, strike!"

He did not tell anybody, not even his nearest comrades, about his "joy of all the afflicted" and it was as though he himself did not know about it,—so deeply was it hidden in his soul. He recalled it but rarely and cautiously.

Now when the terror of the insoluble mystery, which appeared so plainly before him, enveloped him completely, even as the water in high-flood covers the willow twigs on the shore,—a desire came upon him to pray. He felt like kneeling, but he was ashamed of the soldier and, folding his arms on his chest, he whispered softly:

"The joy of all the afflicted!"

And he repeated tenderly, in anguish:

"Joy of all the afflicted, come to me, help Vaska Kashirin."

Long ago, while he was yet in his first term at the university and used to go off on a spree sometimes, before he had made the acquaintance of Werner and before he had entered the organization, he used then to call himself half-boastingly, half-pityingly, "Vaska Kashirin,"—and now for some reason or other he suddenly felt like calling himself by the same name again. But the words had a dead and toneless sound.

"The joy of all the afflicted!"

Something stirred. It was as though some one's calm and mournful image had flashed up in the distance and died out quietly, without illuminating the deathly gloom. The wound-up clock in the steeple struck. The soldier in the corridor made a noise with his gun or with his saber and he yawned, slowly, at intervals.

"Joy of all the afflicted! You are silent! Will you not say anything to Vaska Kashirin?"

He smiled patiently and waited. All was empty within his soul and about him. And the calm, mournful image did not reappear. He recalled, painfully and unnecessarily, wax candles burning; the priest in his vestments; the *ikon* painted on the wall. He recalled his father, bending and stretching himself, praying and bowing to the ground, while looking sidewise to see whether Vaska was praying, or whether he was planning some mischief. And a feeling of still greater terror came over Vasily than before the prayer.

Everything now disappeared.

Madness came crawling painfully. His consciousnesss was dying out like an extinguishing bonfire, growing icy like the corpse of a man who had just died, whose heart is still warm but whose hands and feet had already become stiffened with cold. His dying reason flared up as red as blood again and said that he, Vasily Kashirin, might perhaps become insane here, suffer pains for which there is no name, reach a degree of anguish and suffering that had never been experienced by a single living being; that he might beat his head against the wall, pick his eyes out with his fingers, speak and shout whatever he pleased, that he might plead with tears that he could endure it no longer, —and nothing would happen. Nothing could happen.

And nothing happened. His feet, which had a consciousness and life of their own, continued to walk and to carry his trembling, moist body. His hands, which had a consciousness of their own, endeavored in vain to fasten the coat which was open at his chest and to warm his trembling, moist body.

His body quivered with cold. His eyes stared. And this was calm itself embodied.

But there was one more moment of wild terror. That was when people entered his cell. He did not even imagine that this visit meant that it was time to go to the execution; he simply saw the people and was frightened like a child.

"I will not do it! I will not do it!" he whispered inaudibly with his livid lips and silently retreated to the depth of the cell, even as in childhood he shrank when his father lifted his hand.

"We must start."

The people were speaking, walking around him, handing him something. He closed his eyes, he shook a little,—and began to dress himself slowly. His consciousness must have returned to him, for he suddenly asked the official for a cigarette. And the official generously opened his silver cigarette-case upon which was a chased figure in the style of the decadents.

CHAPTER X

THE WALLS ARE FALLING

THE unidentified man, who called himself Werner, was tired of life and struggle. There was a time when he loved life very dearly, when he enjoyed the theater, literature and social intercourse. Endowed with an excellent memory and a firm will, he had mastered several European languages and could easily pass for a German, a Frenchman or an Englishman. He usually spoke German with a Bavarian accent, but when he felt like it, he could speak like a born Berliner. He was fond of dress, his manners were excellent and he alone, of all the members of the organization, dared attend the balls given in high society, without running the risk of being recognized as an outsider.

But for a long time, altogether unnoticed by his comrades, there had ripened in his soul a dark contempt for mankind; contempt mingled with despair and painful, almost deadly fatigue. By nature rather a mathematician than a poet, he had not known until now any inspiration, any ecstasy and at times he felt like a madman, looking for the squaring of a circle in pools of human blood. The enemy against whom he struggled every day could not inspire him with respect. It was a dense net of stupidity, treachery and falsehood, vile insults and base deceptions. The last incident which seemed to have destroyed in him forever the desire to live, was the murder of the *provocateur* which he had committed by order of the organization. He had killed him in cold blood, but when he saw that dead, deceitful, now calm, and after all pitiful, human face, he suddenly ceased to respect himself and his work. Not that he was seized with a feeling of repentance, but he simply stopped appreciating himself. He became uninteresting to himself, unimportant, a dull stranger. But being a man of strong, unbroken will-power, he did not leave the organization. He remained outwardly the same as before, only there was something cold, yet painful in his eyes. He never spoke to anyone of this.

He possessed another rare quality: just as there are people who have never known headaches, so Werner had never known fear. When other people were afraid, he looked upon them without censure but also without any particular compassion, just as upon a rather contagious illness from which, however, he himself had never suffered. He felt sorry for his comrades, especially for Vasya Kashirin; but that was a cold, almost official pity, which even some of the judges may have felt at times.

Werner understood that the execution was not merely death, that it was something different,—but he resolved to face it calmly, as something not to be considered; to live until the end as if nothing had happened and as if nothing could happen. Only in this way could he express his greatest contempt for capital punishment and preserve his last freedom of the spirit which could not be torn away from him. At the trial—and even his comrades who knew well his cold, haughty fearlessness would perhaps not have believed this,—he thought neither of death nor of life,—but concentrated his attention deeply and coolly upon a difficult chess game which he was playing. A superior chess player, he had started this game on the first day of his imprisonment and continued it uninterruptedly. Even the sentence condemning him to death by hanging did not remove a single figure from his imaginary chessboard.

Even the knowledge that he would not be able to finish this game, did not stop him; and the morning of the last day that he was to remain on earth he started by correcting a not altogether successful move he had made on the previous day. Clasping his lowered hands between his knees, he sat for a long time motionless, then he rose and began to walk, meditating. His walk was peculiar: he leaned the upper part of his body slightly forward and stamped the ground with his heels firmly and distinctly. His steps usually left deep, plain imprints even on dry ground. He whistled softly, in one breath, a simple Italian melody, which helped his meditation.

But this time for some reason or other the thing did not work well. With an unpleasant feeling that he had made some important, even grave blunder, he went back several times and examined the game almost from the beginning. He found no blunder, yet the feeling about a blunder committed not only failed to leave him, but even grew ever more intense and unpleasant. Suddenly an unexpected and offensive thought came into his mind: Did the blunder perhaps consist in his playing chess simply because he wanted to distract his attention from the execution and thus shield himself against the fear of death which is apparently inevitable in every person condemned to death?

"No. What for?" he answered coldly and closed calmly his imaginary chessboard. And with the same concentration with which he had played chess, he tried to give himself an account of the horror and the helplessness of his situation. As though he were going through a strict examination, he looked over the cell, trying not to let anything escape. He counted the hours that remained until the execution, made for himself an approximate and quite exact picture of the execution itself and shrugged his shoulders.

"Well?" he said to some one half-questioningly. "Here it is. Where is the fear?"

Indeed there was no fear. Not only was it not there, but something entirely different, the reverse of fear, developed—a sensation of confused, but enormous and savage joy. And the error, which he had not yet discovered, no longer called forth in him vexation or irritation,—it seemed to speak loudly of something good and unexpected, as though he had believed a dear friend of his to be dead, and that friend turned out to be alive, safe and sound and laughing.

Werner again shrugged his shoulders and felt his pulse,—his heart was beating faster than usual, but soundly and evenly, with a specially ringing throb. He looked about once more, attentively, like a novice for the first time in prison,—examined the walls, the bolts, the chair which was screwed to the floor, and thought:

"Why do I feel so easy, so joyous and free? Yes, so free? I think of the execution to-morrow—and I feel as though it is not there. I look at the walls—and I feel as though they are not here, either. And I feel so free, as though I were not in prison, but had just come out of some prison where I had spent all my life. What does this mean?"

His hands began to tremble,—something Werner had not experienced before. His thoughts fluttered ever more furiously. It was as if tongues of fire had flashed up in his mind, and the fire wanted to burst forth and illumine the distance which was still dark as night. Now the light pierced through and the widely illuminated distance began to shine.

The fatigue that had tormented Werner during the last two years had disappeared; the dead, cold, heavy serpent with its closed eyes and mouth clinched in death, had fallen away from his breast. Before the face of death, beautiful Youth came back to him physically. Indeed, it was more than beautiful Youth. With that wonderful clarity of the spirit which in rare moments comes over man and lifts him to the loftiest peaks of meditation, Werner suddenly perceived both life and death, and he was awed by the splendor of the unprecedented spectacle. It seemed to him that he was walking along the highest mountain-ridge, which was narrow like the blade of a knife, and on one side he saw Life, on the other side—Death,—like two sparkling, deep, beautiful seas, blending in one boundless, broad surface at the horizon.

"What is this? What a divine spectacle!" he said slowly, rising involuntarily and straightening himself, as if in the presence of a supreme being. And destroying the walls, space and time with the impetuosity of his all-penetrating look, he cast a wide glance somewhere into the depth of the life he was to forsake.

And life appeared to him in a new light. He did not strive, as before, to clothe in words that which he had seen; nor were there such words in the still poor, meager human language. That small, cynical and evil feeling which had called forth in him a contempt for mankind and at times even an aversion for the sight of a human face, had disappeared completely. Thus, for a man who goes up in an airship, the filth and litter of the narrow streets disappear and that which was ugly becomes beautiful.

Unconsciously Werner stepped over to the table and leaned his right hand on it. Proud and commanding by nature, he had never before assumed such a proud, free, commanding pose, had never turned his head and never looked as he did now,—for he had never yet been as free and dominant as he was here in the prison, with but a few hours from execution and death.

Now men seemed new to him,—they appeared amiable and charming to his clarified vision. Soaring over time, he saw clearly how young mankind was, that but yesterday it had been howling like a beast in the forests; and that which had seemed to him terrible in human beings, unpardonable and repulsive, suddenly became very dear to him,—like the inability of a child to walk as grown people do, like a child's unconnected lisping, flashing with sparks of genius; like a child's comical blunders, errors and painful bruises.

"My dear people!" Werner suddenly smiled and at once lost all that was imposing in his pose; he again became a prisoner who finds his cell narrow and uncomfortable under lock, and he was tired of the annoying, searching eye staring at him through the peephole in the door. And, strange to say, almost instantly he forgot all that he had seen a little while before so clearly and distinctly; and, what is still stranger, he did not even make an effort to recall it. He simply sat down as comfortably as possible, without the usual stiffness of his body, and surveyed the walls and the bars with a faint and gentle, strange, un-Werner-like smile. Still another new thing happened to Werner, —something that had never happened to him before: he suddenly started to weep.

"My dear comrades!" he whispered, crying bitterly. "My dear comrades!"

By what mysterious ways did he change from the feeling of proud and boundless freedom to this tender and passionate compassion? He did not know, nor did he think of it. Did he pity his dear comrades, or did his tears conceal something else, a still loftier and more passionate feeling?—His suddenly revived and rejuvenated heart did not know this either. He wept and whispered:

"My dear comrades! My dear, dear comrades!"

In this man, who was bitterly weeping and smiling through tears, no one could have recognized the cold and haughty, weary, yet daring Werner—neither the judges, nor the comrades, nor even he himself.

CHAPTER XI

ON THE WAY TO THE SCAFFOLD

BEFORE placing the condemned people in coaches, all five were brought together in a large cold room with a vaulted ceiling, which resembled an office, where people worked no longer, or a deserted waiting-room. They were now permitted to speak to one another.

Only Tanya Kovalchuk availed herself at once of the permission. The others firmly and silently shook each other's hands, which were as cold as ice and as hot as fire,—and silently, trying not to look at each other, they crowded together in an awkward, absent-minded group. Now that they were together, they felt somewhat ashamed of what each of them had experienced when alone; and they were afraid to look, so as not to notice or to show that new, peculiar, somewhat shameful sensation that each of them felt or suspected the others of feeling.

But after a short silence they glanced at each other, smiled and immediately began to feel at ease and unrestrained, as before. No change seemed to have occurred, and if it had occurred, it had come so gently over all of them that it could not be discerned in any one separately. All spoke and moved about strangely: abruptly, by jolts, either too fast or too slowly. Sometimes they seemed to choke with their words and repeated them a number of times; sometimes they did not finish a phrase they had started, or thought they had finished—they did not notice it. They all blinked their eyes and examined ordinary objects curiously, not recognizing them, like people who had worn eye-glasses and had suddenly taken them off; and all of them frequently turned around abruptly, as though some one behind them was calling them all the time and showing them something. But they did not notice this, either. Musya's and Tanya Kovalchuk's cheeks and ears were burning; Sergey was at first somewhat pale, but he soon recovered and looked as he always did.

Only Vasily attracted everybody's attention. Even among them, he looked strange and terrible. Werner became agitated and said to Musya in a low voice, with tender anxiety:

"What does this mean, Musyechka? Is it possible that he—— What? I must go to him."

Vasily looked at Werner from the distance, as though not recognizing him, and he lowered his eyes.

"Vasya, what have you done with your hair? What is the matter with you? Never mind, my dear, never mind, it will soon be over. We must keep up, we must, we must."

Vasily was silent. But when it seemed that he would no longer say anything, a dull, belated, terribly remote answer came—like an answer from the grave:

"I'm all right. I hold my own."

Then he repeated:

"I hold my own."

Werner was delighted.

"That's the way, that's the way. Good boy. That's the way."

But his eyes met Vasily's dark, wearied glance fixed upon him from the distance and he thought with instant sorrow: "From where is he looking? From where is he speaking?" and with profound tenderness, with which people address a grave, he said:

"Vasya, do you hear? I love you very much."

"So do I love you very much," answered the tongue, moving with difficulty.

Suddenly Musya took Werner by the hand and with an expression of surprise, she said like an actress on the stage, with measured emphasis:

"Werner, what is this? You said, 'I love'? You never before said 'I love' to anybody. And why are you all so—tender and serene? Why?"

"Why?"

And like an actor, also accentuating what he felt, Werner pressed Musya's hand firmly:

"Yes, now I love very much. Don't tell it to the others,—it isn't necessary, I feel somewhat ashamed, but I love deeply."

Their eyes met and flashed up brightly, and everything about them seemed to have plunged in darkness. It is thus that in the flash of lightning all other lights are instantly darkened and the heavy yellow flame casts a shadow upon earth.

"Yes," said Musya, "yes, Werner."

"Yes," he answered, "yes, Musya, yes."

They understood each other and something was firmly settled between them at this moment. And his eyes glistening, Werner again became agitated and quickly stepped over to Sergey.

"Seryozha!"

But Tanya Kovalchuk answered. Almost crying with maternal pride, she tugged Sergey frantically by the sleeve.

"Listen, Werner! I am crying here for him, I am wearing myself to death, and he is occupying himself with gymnastics!"

"According to the Müller system?" smiled Werner.

Sergey knit his brow confusedly.

"You needn't laugh, Werner. I have convinced myself conclusively——"

All began to laugh. Drawing strength and courage from one another, they gradually regained their poise—became the same as they used to be. They did not notice this, however, and thought that they had never changed at all. Suddenly Werner interrupted their laughter and said to Sergey very earnestly:

"You are right, Seryozha. You are perfectly right."

"No, but you must understand," said Golovin gladly. "Of course, we——"

But at this point they were asked to start. And their jailers were so kind as to permit them to ride in pairs, as they pleased. Altogether the jailers were extremely kind; even too kind. It was as if they tried partly to show themselves humane and partly to show that they were not there at all, but that everything was being done as by machinery. But they were all pale.

"Musya, you go with him." Werner pointed at Vasily, who stood motionless.

"I understand," Musya nodded. "And you?"

"I? Tanya will go with Sergey, you go with Vasya. . . . I will go alone. That doesn't matter, I can do it, you know."

When they went out in the yard, the moist, soft darkness rushed warmly and strongly against their faces, their eyes, taking their breath away, then suddenly it penetrated their bodies tenderly and refreshingly. It was hard to believe that this wonderful effect was produced simply by the spring wind, the warm, moist wind. And the really wonderful spring night was filled with the odor of melting snow, and through the boundless space the noise of drops resounded. Hastily and frequently, as though trying to overtake one another, little drops were falling, striking in unison a ringing tune. Suddenly one of them would strike out of tune and all was mingled in a merry splash in hasty confusion. Then a large, heavy drop would strike firmly and again the fast, spring melody resounded distinctly. And over the city, above the roofs of the fortress, hung a pale redness in the sky reflected by the electric lights.

"U-ach!" Sergey Golovin heaved a deep sigh and held his breath, as though he regretted to exhale from his lungs the fine, fresh air.

"How long have you had such weather?" inquired Werner. "It's real spring."

"It's only the second day," was the polite answer. "Before that we had mostly frosty weather."

The dark carriages rolled over noiselessly one after another, took them in by twos, started off into the darkness—there where the lantern was shaking at the gate. The convoys like gray silhouettes surrounded each carriage; the horseshoes struck noisily against the ground, or plashed upon the melting snow.

When Werner bent down, about to climb into the carriage, the gendarme whispered to him:

"There is somebody else going along with you."

Werner was surprised.

"Where? Where is he going? Oh, yes! Another one? Who is he?"

The gendarme was silent. Indeed, in a dark corner a small, motionless but living figure pressed close to the side of the carriage. By the reflection of the lantern Werner noticed the flash of an open eye. Seating himself, Werner pushed his foot against the other man's knee.

"Excuse me, comrade."

The man made no reply. It was only when the carriage started, that he suddenly asked in broken Russian, speaking with difficulty:

"Who are you?"

"I am Werner, condemned to hanging for the attempt upon N—. And you?"

"I am Yanson. They must not hang me."

They were riding thus in order to appear two hours later face to face before the inexplicable great mystery, in order to pass from Life to Death—and they were introducing each other. Life and Death moved simultaneously, and until the very end Life remained life, to the most ridiculous and insipid trifles.

"What have you done, Yanson?"

"I killed my master with a knife. I stole money."

It seemed from the tone of his voice that Yanson was falling asleep. Werner found his flabby hand in the darkness and pressed it. Yanson withdrew it drowsily.

"Are you afraid?" asked Werner.

"I don't want to be hanged."

They became silent. Werner again found the Esthonian's hand and pressed it firmly between his dry, burning palms. Yanson's hand lay motionless, like a board, but he made no longer any effort to withdraw it.

It was close and suffocating in the carriage. The air was filled with the smell of soldiers' clothes, mustiness, and the leather of wet boots. The young gendarme who sat opposite Werner breathed warmly upon him, and in his breath there was the odor of onions and cheap tobacco. But some brisk, fresh air came in through certain clefts, and because of this, spring was felt even more intensely in this small, stifling, moving box, than outside. The carriage kept turning now to the right, now to the left, now it seemed to turn back. At times it seemed as though they had been turning around on one and the same spot for hours for some reason or other. At first a bluish electric light penetrated through the lowered, heavy window shades; then suddenly, after a certain turn it grew dark, and only by this could they guess that they had turned into deserted streets in the outskirts of the city and that they were nearing the S. railroad station. Sometimes during sharp turns, Werner's live, bent knee would strike against the live, bent knee of the gendarme, and it was hard to believe that the execution was approaching.

"Where are we going?" Yanson asked suddenly. He was somewhat dizzy from the continuous turning of the dark box and he felt slightly sick at his stomach.

Werner answered and pressed the Esthonian's hand more firmly. He felt like saying something especially kind and caressing to this little, sleepy man, and he already loved him as he had never loved anyone in his life.

"You don't seem to sit comfortably, my dear man. Move over here, to me."

Yanson was silent for awhile, then he replied:

"Well, thank you. I'm sitting all right. Are they going to hang you too?"

"Yes," answered Werner, almost laughing with unexpected jollity, and he waved his hand easily and freely, as though he were speaking of some absurd and trifling joke which kind but terribly comical people wanted to play on him.

"Have you a wife?" asked Yanson.

"No. I have no wife. I am single."

"I am also alone. Alone," said Yanson.

Werner's head also began to feel dizzy. And at times it seemed that they were going to some festival; strange to say, almost all those who went to the scaffold experienced the same sensation and mingled with sorrow and fear there was a vague joy as they anticipated the extraordinary thing that was soon to befall them. Reality was intoxicated with madness and Death, united with Life, brought forth apparitions. It seemed very possible that flags were waving over the houses.

"We have arrived!" said Werner gayly when the carriage stopped, and he jumped out easily. But with Yanson it was a rather slow affair: silently and very drowsily he resisted and would not come out. He seized the knob. The gendarme opened the weak fingers and pulled his hand away. Then Yanson seized the corner of the carriage, the door, the high wheel, but immediately let it go upon the slightest effort on the part of the gendarme. He did not exactly seize these things; he rather cleaved to each object sleepily and silently, and was torn away easily, without any effort. Finally he got up.

There were no flags. The railroad station was dark, deserted and lifeless; the passenger trains were not running any longer, and the train which was silently waiting for these passengers on the way needed no bright light, no commotion. Suddenly Werner began to feel weary. It was not fear, nor anguish, but a feeling of enormous, painful, tormenting weariness which makes one feel like going off somewhere, lying down and closing one's eyes very tightly. Werner stretched himself and yawned slowly. Yanson also stretched himself and quickly yawned several times.

"I wish they'd be quicker about it," said Werner wearily. Yanson was silent, shrinking together.

When the condemned moved along the deserted platform which was surrounded by soldiers, to the dimly lighted cars, Werner found himself near Sergey Golovin; Sergey, pointing with his hand somewhere aside, began to say something, but only the word "lantern" was heard distinctly, and the rest was drowned in slow and weary yawning.

"What did you say?" asked Werner, also yawning.

"The lantern. The lamp in the lantern is smoking," said Sergey. Werner looked around. Indeed, the lamp in the lantern was smoking very much, and the glass had already turned black on top.

"Yes, it is smoking."

Suddenly he thought: "What have I to do with the smoking of the lamp, since——"

Sergey apparently thought the same, as he glanced quickly at Werner and turned away. But both stopped yawning.

They all went to the cars themselves, only Yanson had to be led by the arms. At first he stamped his feet and his boots seemed to stick to the boards of the platform. Then he bent his knees and fell into the arms of the gendarmes, his feet dangled like those of a very intoxicated man, and the tips of the boots scraped against the wood. It took a long time until he was silently pushed through the door.

Vasily Kashirin also moved himself, unconsciously imitating the movements of his comrades—he did everything as they did. But on boarding the platform of the car, he stumbled, and a gendarme took him by the elbow to support him. Vasily shuddered and screamed shrilly, drawing back his arm:

"Ai!"

"What is it, Vasya?" Werner rushed over to him. Vasily was silent, trembling in every limb. The confused and even offended gendarme explained:

"I wanted to keep him from falling, and he——"

"Come, Vasya, let me hold you," said Werner, about to take him by the arm. But Vasily drew back his arm again and cried more loudly than before:

"Ai!"

"Vasya, it is I, Werner."

"I know. Don't touch me. I'll go myself."

And continuing to tremble he entered the car himself and seated himself in a corner. Bending over to Musya, Werner asked her softly, pointing with his eyes at Vasily:

"How about him?"

"Bad," answered Musya, also in a soft voice. "He is dead already. Werner, tell me, is there such a thing as death?"

"I don't know, Musya, but I think that there is no such thing," replied Werner seriously and thoughtfully.

"That's what I have thought. But he? I was tortured with him in the carriage—it was like riding with a corpse."

"I don't know, Musya. Perhaps there is such a thing as death for some people. Meanwhile, perhaps, but later there will be no death. For me death also existed before, but now it exists no longer."

Musya's somewhat paled cheeks flushed as she asked:

"It did exist, Werner? It did?"

"It did. But not now any longer. Just the same as with you."

A noise was heard in the doorway of the car. Mishka Tsiganok entered, stamping noisily with his heels, breathing loudly and spitting. He cast a swift glance and stopped obdurately.

"No room here, gendarme!" he shouted to the tired gendarme who looked at him angrily. "You make it so that I am comfortable here, otherwise I won't go—hang me here on the lamp-post. What a carriage they gave me, dogs! Is that a carriage? It's the devil's belly, not a carriage!"

But suddenly he bent down his head, stretched out his neck and thus went forward to the others. Out of the disheveled frame of hair and beard his black eyes looked wildly and sharply with an almost insane expression.

"Ah, gentlemen!" he drawled out. "So that's what it is. Hello, master!"

He thrust his hand to Werner and sat down opposite him. And bending closely over to him, he winked one eye and quickly passed his hand over his throat.

"You, too? What?"

"Yes!" smiled Werner.

"Are all of us to be hanged?"

"All."

"Oho!" Tsiganok grinned, showing his teeth, and quickly felt everybody with his eyes, stopping for an instant longer on Musya and Yanson. Then he winked again to Werner.

"The Minister?"

"Yes, the Minister. And you?"

"I am here for something else, master. People like me don't deal with ministers. I am a murderer, master, that's what I am. An ordinary murderer. Never mind, master, move away a little, I haven't come into your company of my own will. There will be room enough for all of us in the other world."

He surveyed them all with one swift, suspicious, wild glance from under his disheveled hair. But all looked at him silently and seriously, even with apparent interest. He grinned, showing his teeth, and quickly clapped Werner on the knee several times.

"That's the way, master! How does the song run? 'Don't rustle, O green little mother forest. . . .' "

"Why do you call me 'master,' since we are all going——"

"Correct," Tsiganok agreed with satisfaction. "What kind of master are you, if you are going to hang right beside me? There is a master for you"; and he pointed with his finger at the silent gendarme. "Eh, that fellow there is not worse than our kind"; he pointed with his eyes at Vasily. "Master! Eh there, master! You're afraid, aren't you?"

"No," answered the heavy tongue.

"Never mind that 'No.' Don't be ashamed; there's nothing to be ashamed of. Only a dog wags his tail and snarls when he is taken to be hanged, but you are a man. Who is that dope? He isn't one of you, is he?"

He darted his glance rapidly about, and hissing, kept spitting continuously. Yanson, curled up into a motionless bundle, pressed closely into the corner. The flaps of his outworn fur cap stirred, but he maintained silence. Werner answered for him:

"He killed his employer."

"O Lord!" wondered Tsiganok. "Why are such people allowed to kill?"

For some time Tsiganok had been looking sideways at Musya; now turning quickly, he stared at her sharply, straight into her face.

"Young lady, young lady! What about

you? Her cheeks are rosy and she is laughing. Look, she is really laughing," he said, clasping Werner's knee with his clutching, iron-like fingers. "Look, look!"

Reddening, smiling confusedly, Musya also gazed straight into his sharp and wildly searching eyes.

The wheels rattled fast and noisily. The small cars kept hopping along the narrow rails. Now at a curve or at a crossing the small engine whistled shrilly and carefully —the engineer was afraid lest he might run over somebody. It was strange to think that so much humane painstaking care and exertion was being introduced into the business of hanging people; that the most insane deed on earth was being committed with such an air of simplicity and reasonableness. The cars were running, and human beings sat in them as people always do, and they rode as people usually ride; and then there would be a halt, as usual.

"The train will stop for five minutes."

And there death would be waiting—eternity—the great mystery.

CHAPTER XII

THEY ARE HANGED

THE little cars ran on carefully.

Sergey Golovin at one time had lived for several years with his relatives at their country-house, along this very road. He had traveled upon it by day as well as by night, and he knew it well. He closed his eyes, and thought that he might now simply be returning home—that he had stayed out late in the city with acquaintances, and was now coming back on the last train.

"We will soon be there," he said, opening his eyes and looking out of the grated, mute window.

Nobody stirred, nobody answered; only Tsiganok spat quickly several times and his eyes ran over the car, as though feeling the windows, the doors, the soldiers.

"It's cold," said Vasily Kashirin, his lips closed tightly, as though really frozen; and his words sounded strangely.

Tanya Kovalchuk began to bustle about.

"Here's a handkerchief. Tie it about your neck. It's a very warm one."

"Around the neck?" Sergey asked suddenly, startled by his own question. But as the same thing occurred to all of them, no one seemed to hear him. It was as if nothing had been said, or as if they had all said the same thing at the same time.

"Never mind, Vasya, tie it about your neck. It will be warmer," Werner advised him. Then he turned to Yanson and asked gently:

"And you, friend, are you cold?"

"Werner, perhaps he wants to smoke. Comrade, perhaps you would like to smoke?" asked Musya. "We have something to smoke."

"I do."

"Give him a cigarette, Seryozha," said Werner delightedly. But Sergey was already getting out a cigarette. All looked on with friendliness, watching how Yanson's fingers took the cigarette, how the match flared, and then how the blue smoke issued from Yanson's mouth.

"Thanks," said Yanson; "it's good."

"How strange!" said Sergey.

"What is strange?" Werner turned around. "What is strange?"

"I mean—the cigarette."

Yanson held a cigarette, an ordinary cigarette, in his ordinary live hands, and, pale-faced, looked at it with surprise, even with terror. And all fixed their eyes upon the little tube, from the end of which smoke was issuing, like a bluish ribbon, wafted aside by the breathing, with the ashes, gathering, turning black. The light went out.

"The light's out," said Tanya.

"Yes, the light's out."

"Let it go," said Werner, frowning, looking uneasily at Yanson, whose hand, holding the cigarette, was hanging loosely, as if dead. Suddenly Tsiganok turned quickly, bent over to Werner, close to him, face to face, and rolling the whites of his eyes, like a horse, whispered:

"Master, how about the convoys? Suppose we—eh? Shall we try?"

"No, don't do it," Werner replied, also in a whisper. "We shall drink it to the bitter end."

"Why not? It's livelier in a fight! Eh? I strike him, he strikes me, and you don't even know how the thing is done. It's just as if you don't die at all."

"No, you shouldn't do it," said Werner, and turned to Yanson. "Why don't you smoke, friend?"

Suddenly Yanson's wizened face became wofully wrinkled, as if somebody had pulled strings which set all the wrinkles in motion. And, as in a dream, he began to whimper, without tears, in a dry, strained voice:

"I don't want to smoke. Aha! aha! aha! Why should I be hanged? Aha! aha! aha!"

They began to bustle about him. Tanya Kovalchuk, weeping freely, petted him on the arm, and adjusted the drooping earlaps of his worn fur cap.

"My dear, do not cry! My own! my dear! Poor, unfortunate little fellow!"

Musya looked aside. Tsiganok caught her glance and grinned, showing his teeth.

"What a queer fellow! He drinks tea, and yet feels cold," he said, with an abrupt laugh. But suddenly his own face became bluish-black, like cast-iron, and his large yellow teeth flashed.

Suddenly the little cars trembled and slackened their speed. All, except Yanson and Kashirin, rose and sat down again quickly.

"Here is the station," said Sergey.

It seemed to them as if all the air had been suddenly pumped out of the car, it became so difficult to breathe. The heart grew larger, making the chest almost burst, beating in the throat, tossing about madly—shouting in horror with its blood-filled voice. And the eyes looked upon the quivering floor, and the ears heard how the wheels were turning ever more slowly—the wheels slipped and turned again, and then suddenly—they stopped.

The train had halted.

Then a dream set in. It was not terrible, rather fantastic, unfamiliar to the memory, strange. The dreamer himself seemed to remain aside, only his bodiless apparition moved about, spoke soundlessly, walked noiselessly, suffered without suffering. As in a dream, they walked out of the car, formed into parties of two, inhaled the peculiarly fresh spring air of the forest. As in a dream, Yanson resisted bluntly, powerlessly, and was dragged out of the car silently.

They descended the steps of the station.

"Are we to walk?" asked some one almost cheerily.

"It isn't far now," answered another, also cheerily.

Then they walked in a large, black, silent crowd amid the forest, along a rough, wet and soft spring road. From the forest, from the snow, a fresh, strong breath of air was wafted. The feet slipped, sometimes sinking into the snow, and involuntarily the hands of the comrades clung to each other. And the convoys, breathing with difficulty, walked over the untouched snow on each side of the road. Some one said in an angry voice:

"Why didn't they clear the road? Did they want us to turn somersaults in the snow?"

Some one else apologized guiltily.

"We cleaned it, your Honor. But it is thawing and it can't be helped."

Consciousness of what they were doing returned to the prisoners, but not completely, —in fragments, in strange parts. Now, suddenly, their minds practically admitted:

"It is indeed impossible to clear the road."

Then again everything died out, and only their sense of smell remained: the unbearably fresh smell of the forest and of the melting snow. And everything became unusually clear to the consciousness: the forest, the night, the road and the fact that soon they would be hanged. Their conversation, restrained to whispers, flashed in fragments.

"It is almost four o'clock."

"I said we started too early."

"The sun dawns at five."

"Of course, at five. We should have——"

They stopped in a meadow, in the darkness. A little distance away, beyond the bare trees, two small lanterns moved silently. There were the gallows.

"I lost one of my rubbers," said Sergey Golovin.

"Really?" asked Werner, not understanding what he said.

"I lost a rubber. It's cold."

"Where's Vasily?"

"I don't know. There he is."

Vasily stood, gloomy, motionless.

"And where is Musya?"

"Here I am. Is that you, Werner?"

They began to look about, avoiding the direction of the gallows, where the lanterns continued to move about silently with terrible suggestiveness. On the left, the bare forest seemed to be growing thinner, and something large and white and flat was visible. A damp wind issued from it.

"The sea," said Sergey Golovin, inhaling

the air with nose and mouth. "The sea is there!"

Musya answered sonorously:

"My love which is as broad as the sea!"

"What is that, Musya?"

"The banks of life cannot hold my love, which is as broad as the sea."

"My love which is as broad as the sea," echoed Sergey, thoughtfully, carried away by the sound of her voice and by her words.

"My love which is as broad as the sea," repeated Werner, and suddenly he spoke wonderingly, cheerfully:

"Musya, how young you are!"

Suddenly Tsiganok whispered warmly, out of breath, right into Werner's ear:

"Master! master! There's the forest! My God! what's that? There—where the lanterns are—are those the gallows? What does it mean?"

Werner looked at him. Tsiganok was writhing in agony before his death.

"We must bid each other good-by," said Tanya Kovalchuk.

"Wait, they have yet to read the sentence," answered Werner. "Where is Yanson?"

Yanson was lying on the snow, and about him people were busying themselves. There was a smell of ammonia in the air.

"Well, what is it, doctor? Will you be through soon?" some one asked impatiently.

"It's nothing. He has simply fainted. Rub his ears with snow! He is coming to himself already! You may read the sentence!"

The light of the dark lantern flashed upon the paper and on the white, gloveless hands holding it. Both the paper and the hands quivered slightly, and the voice also quivered:

"Gentlemen, perhaps it is not necessary to read the sentence to you. You know it already. What do you say?"

"Don't read it," Werner answered for them all, and the little lantern was soon extinguished.

The services of the priest were also declined by them all. Tsiganok said:

"Stop your fooling, father—you will forgive me, but they will hang me. Go to—where you came from."

And the dark, broad silhouette of the priest moved back silently and quickly and disappeared. Day was breaking: the snow turned whiter, the figures of the people became more distinct, and the forest—thinner, more melancholy.

"Gentlemen, you must go in pairs. Take your places in pairs as you wish, but I ask you to hurry up."

Werner pointed to Yanson, who was now standing, supported by two gendarmes.

"I will go with him. And you, Seryozha, take Vasily. Go ahead."

"Very well."

"You and I go together, Musechka, shall we not?" asked Tanya Kovalchuk. "Come, let us kiss each other good-by."

They kissed one another quickly. Tsiganok kissed firmly, so that they felt his teeth; Yanson softly, drowsily, with his mouth half open—and it seemed that he did not understand what he was doing.

When Sergey Golovin and Kashirin had

gone a few steps, Kashirin suddenly stopped and said loudly and distinctly:

"Good-by, comrades."

"Good-by, comrade," they shouted in answer.

They went off. It grew quiet. The lanterns beyond the trees became motionless. They awaited an outcry, a voice, some kind of noise—but it was just as quiet there as it was among them—and the yellow lanterns were motionless.

"Oh, my God!" some one cried hoarsely and wildly. They looked about. It was Tsiganok, writhing in agony at the thought of death. "They are hanging!"

They turned away from him, and again it became quiet. Tsiganok was writhing, catching at the air with his hands.

"How is that, gentlemen? Am I to go alone? It's livelier to die together. Gentlemen, what does it mean?"

He seized Werner by the hand, his fingers clutching and then relaxing.

"Dear master, at least you come with me? Eh? Do me the favor? Don't refuse."

Werner answered painfully:

"I can't, my dear fellow. I am going with him."

"Oh, my God! Must I go alone, then? My God! How is it to be?"

Musya stepped forward and said softly:

"You may go with me."

Tsiganok stepped back and rolled the whites of his eyes wildly.

"With you!"

"Yes."

"Just think of her! What a little girl! And you're not afraid? If you are, I would rather go alone!"

"No, I am not afraid."

Tsiganok grinned.

"Just think of her! But do you know that I am a murderer? Don't you despise me? You had better not do it. I shan't be angry at you."

Musya was silent, and in the faint light of dawn her face was pale and enigmatic. Then suddenly she walked over to Tsiganok quickly, and, throwing her arms about his neck, kissed him firmly upon his lips. He took her by the shoulders with his fingers, held her away from himself, then shook her, and, with loud smacks, kissed her on the lips, on the nose, on the eyes.

"Come!"

Suddenly the soldier standing nearest them staggered forward, and opening his hands, let his gun drop. He did not stoop down to regain it, but stood for an instant motionless, turned abruptly and, like a blind man, walked toward the forest over the untouched snow.

"Where are you going?" called out another soldier in fright. "Halt!"

But the man continued walking through the deep snow silently and with difficulty. Then he must have stumbled over something, for he waved his arms and fell face downward. And there he remained lying on the snow.

"Pick up the gun, you sour-faced graycoat, or I'll pick it up," said Tsiganok sternly to the other soldier. "You don't know your business!"

The little lanterns began to move about

busily again. Now it was the turn of Werner and Yanson.

"Good-by, master!" called Tsiganok loudly. "We'll meet each other in the other world, you'll see! Don't turn away from me. When you see me, bring me some water to drink—it will be hot there for me!"

"Good-by!"

"I don't want to be hanged!" said Yanson drowsily.

Werner took him by the hand, and then the Esthonian walked a few steps alone. But later they saw him stop and fall down in the snow. Soldiers bent over him, lifted him up and carried him on, and he struggled faintly in their arms. Why did he not cry? He must have forgotten even that he had a voice.

And again the little yellow lanterns became motionless.

"And I, Musechka," said Tanya Kovalchuk mournfully, "must I go alone? We lived together, and now——"

"Tanechka, dearest——"

But Tsiganok took her part heatedly.

Holding her by the hand, as though fearing that some one would take her away from him, he said quickly, in a business-like manner, to Tanya:

"Ah, young lady, you can go alone! You are a pure soul—you can go alone wherever you please! But I—I can't! A murderer! . . . Understand? I can't go alone! Where are you going, you murderer? they will ask me. Why, I even stole horses, by God! But with her it is just as if —just as if I were with an infant, understand? Do you understand me?"

"I do. Go. Come, let me kiss you once more, Musechka."

"Kiss! Kiss each other!" urged Tsiganok. "That's a woman's job! You must bid each other a hearty good-by!"

Musya and Tsiganok moved forward. Musya walked cautiously, slipping, and by force of habit raising her skirts slightly. And the man led her to death firmly, holding her arm carefully and feeling the ground with his foot.

The lights stopped moving. It was quiet

and lonely around Tanya Kovalchuk. The soldiers were silent, all gray in the soft, colorless light of daybreak.

"I am alone," sighed Tanya Kovalchuk suddenly. "Seryozha is dead, Werner is dead—and Vasya, too. I am alone! Soldiers! soldiers! I am alone, alone——"

The sun was rising over the sea.

The bodies were placed in a box. Then they were taken away. With stretched necks, with bulging eyes, with blue, swollen tongues, looking like some unknown, terrible flowers between the lips, which were covered with bloody foam—the bodies were hurried back along the same road by which they had come—alive. And the spring snow was just as soft and fresh; the spring air was just as strong and fragrant. And on the snow lay Sergey's black rubber-shoe, wet, trampled under foot.

Thus did men greet the rising sun.

THE END